The Predator

The Making Of A Wiseguy

A Novel
By
Anthony V. Aqua

Contact the author at: donricciwiseguy@aol.com
Join the Fan Discussion at: www.facebook.com/DonRicciWiseGuy

Stock imagery is being used for illustrative purposes only. Image of mask for cover illustration provided by Rusak/Bigstock.com.

ISBN: 149486651X
ISBN 13: 9781494866518

Dedication

This book is dedicated to the men and women who are enslaved around the world in the sex trade.

Attention must be given to the disappeared, who are taken advantage of in mind, body, and soul. Their captors mean for them to feel lost and without hope of rescue. That is far from the truth, however, as many people are out there looking for them and wanting to help them.

I encourage the missing to call out for help, just the way the woman with the child did in Cleveland, Ohio.

Prologue:
The Turning Point

It was midnight when George heard the cleaning crew. In broken English, Jose asked, "Excuse por favor, Mister Ricci, it okay empty your basket and vacuum?"

"Sure, sure, Jose, I lost track of time."

"Mister Ricci, you go, you go home, this snowstorm a killer."

George looked out the window as he picked up and organized his papers, placing them in the locking filing cabinets before hastily beating a departure down the elevator to the parking garage. George turned left onto Charles from Beacon Street, jumping onto Storrow Drive that follows the Charles River in Boston.

George and Mary had purchased a home on Gloucester Bay. Mary and little Donny had everything they wanted. His family would relax at the boat and golf club, the spa, and lived in the lap of luxury. They seemed to live an enchanted life.

Turning onto Route 128 North, he would be home in fifteen miles, but the roads had gotten worse.

George thought, *Can you imagine no rock salt on the road in this snow? With all of the taxes in Taxachusetts, we should at least have rock salt.*

The driving posed him no problem, until he went over an iced-up steel bridge. The Mercedes-Benz started to spin ever so slowly. George could do absolutely nothing about it. The car went out of control as the ice took it spinning.

George called out, "Oh God, help me!" The words came automatically and instantly out of his mouth; he didn't have to think or react. "Mama, Mama, please help me!" He was not calling for his birth mother but to his spiritual Mother to save him.

There was a loud thump, and the car started to rise into the air, tumbling over uncontrollably until it stopped with a splash in the marsh.

"Thank God!" he heard himself say, as he lay there disoriented, his head pounding. Blood blurred his vision. His legs were pinned under the dash; he simply could not move. His right shoulder blade was broken.

"Oh my God, I am so tired." George drifted into unconsciousness.

Then the morning sun warmed his face. "That feels so good," he said.

He awoke thinking he was home in bed, and he'd had a bad nightmare. He thought the sun was streaming through the curtains of the bedroom deck wraparound window.

But then he had to fight to open his eyes that were now stuck closed with dried blood. His sports car had come to rest on its left side in a tidal salt marsh so close to home. But time and tides wait for no man, and this certainly proved true for George Ricci.

The tide inched its way into the car, and George felt the cold liquid lapping at his left ear. It was the kiss of death. Salt water burned George's open cuts, snapping him back to reality.

Water slowly trickled into his nose and mouth with each breath. He coughed and gasped for air as the car filled with the frigid water. He cried out, "Mary, I love you so much." George stopped breathing, but he could still see Mary and Donald, until they slowly faded from view.

Three days later, a hunter looking for some pheasant to grace his dinner plate wandered through the salt marsh at low tide. He placed his double-barrel twelve gauge Remington shotgun on a large bolder by the water before he approached the car, peering through the cracked windshield to see someone lying on his side.

"Hey mister, hey, you okay?"

There was no reply. The only thing he heard were the chirps of some chickadees as they also called out to the body lying inside the car. The date was January 14, 1988.

Donald was ten years old.

George left his family a life insurance policy valued at $5 million, a fully paid house plus a substantial stock portfolio, but these things were a poor substitute for the firm but loving guidance of a father. George's death changed Don for life, forever, and not for the better.

Mary languished for months, lying in bed trying to decide what to do. She sent Donny away to boarding school immediately after the accident, just when he needed his mother the most. He didn't even get to say goodbye to his school friends, not even his best friend whom he'd known since kindergarten.

Then one day Mary sat up in bed and swore she heard George say clear as a bell, "Well, Babe, das is das, life must go on, enjoy it."

She remarried within the year, to her son's devastation.

Don withdrew into a shell of anger. He became aggressive and would lash out whenever he felt justified to do so. It was his way or no way. This attitude would get him into trouble more times than he really cared for, but he never saw the light of day.

So despite coming from a good family, Don grew into a man with a warped sense of right and wrong.

One

Tonight's the Night

Don Ricci sat in his living room around sunset, drinking boilermakers and watching porn. He liked the vintage stuff from the golden age of porn, from before he was born. He watched as Linda Lovelace went down on John Holmes, taking it all the way down her throat until she was sucking on his balls. After reaching orgasm, he made the decision, *Tonight ... tonight's definitely the night.*

He started to fantasize, visualizing erotic happenings. *Could you imagine what it would be like to be on a desert island with twenty girls? I would be a king with a harem. They would fight among themselves with the winner eagerly wanting to please me. She would submit to my every thought and desire, as well as suggesting things that I could not even think of, sending me into ecstasy.*

Closing his eyes, he invoked images of Julie. But he'd had too much to drink, and he fell into a restless dream world. At 2 a.m., he turned over and rolled off of the couch, hitting his head on the floor. Jumping up, his eyes bulged wide open with fear as he tried to locate where he was and what had made the noise. He couldn't remember his nightmare as he sat down on the couch.

Don lit up and inhaled deeply on his cigarette, trying to remember as his mind cleared. "Damn it!"

He put on his sneakers and headed to the cellar stairs to retrieve everything he'd need. He had put it all into an old wooden milk crate with faded white lettering – WHITTLINGS MILK COMPANY. Attached to the crate by way of black masking tape was a list of the contents with a check mark beside each item. Transferring a generous amount of chloroform into a small glass bottle, he secured it in his right-hand jacket pocket. Don thought of himself as a very meticulous person – he thought he was not prone to making mistakes.

Unlocking the entrance to the bulkhead, he placed the padlock on the table and picked up the box of supplies. He placed them in the shiny red wheelbarrow that had two wheels on the front for the best balance possible. No matter how much weight, he would not lose control. Don didn't like to lose control.

On the stairwell going out of the cellar, Don had placed an eight-inch wide plank over each side of the steps. This would make it a snap to pull or push the wheelbarrow and ride his "ill-gotten gains" down into the cellar. He pushed the wheelbarrow up the ramp by stepping between the planks and slid it smoothly onto the grass.

Reaching down for a string near the hinge of the bulkhead going down to the basement, he pulled it, turning off the light. He left the cellar doors open so as not to make any additional noise. After all, he'd be back soon; she lived only two and a half miles away.

When he got to the curb, he stayed on the sidewalk. Moving noiselessly, he turned his head right and left, making sure he wasn't spotted by anyone up at this time of night.

His stealthy gait was not a run but an evenly timed cadence so he wouldn't overtax himself.

He wore a Boston Red Sox cap two sizes too big, pulled down over his ears to hide his black, curly hair and handsome features. At age 32, Don stood at six-three and weighed in at just a shade over 220 of pure muscle. Everything Don wore was black to blend into his surroundings. He felt safe and smug, except there were things outside of his control. Spring in Massachusetts typically wasn't this warm. *Fuck, all the dogs in the neighborhood are chained to their damn back porches to keep 'em cool tonight*, he silently fumed.

A symphony of barking escorted Don down the street on his quest. Finally, after getting a block away, the sound of the dogs faded, and Don decided to slow down. *I must reserve my strength ... I'll need it very shortly.*

The new handicapped wheelchair ramps the town had installed at each crosswalk were a blessing to his escapade, since all of the colonial homes were built before the second world war at a time when there were no particular laws to champion the disabled. The large tube tires of his wheelbarrow just glided down and up with no effort at all. He had considered driving, but decided using the wheelbarrow was safer because it would make no engine noise, was easier to conceal, and it did not have license plates to trace.

He made a right turn down Pine Hill, a left on Gillis, then onto Mohawk, Julie's street. The night was dark as mud, without a moon at all.

He used a small flashlight, meticulously checking the numbers on the mailboxes. "Sweetheart, daddy's coming,"

Don had been on the move nearly thirty minutes as he approached Julie's home, and he was out of breath. He grunted to himself, "69 Mohawk ... here I am."

Two

Julie's Home

Don pushed the wheelbarrow up the driveway and stopped right by the rear steps, sitting down to catch his breath and renew his strength. Reaching into the left pocket of his jacket, he retrieved his rubber gloves before grabbing a candy bar from his right pocket. He snapped it into his mouth and salivated as the taste of dark chocolate melted on his tongue. He swallowed; flashing back to the night in high school he met a wild Irish girl at Nahant Beach.

She had enormous tits. Her hair was short and curly, almost like an Afro. She took Don away from the beach party to the parking lot and her car. Opening the door to the back seat and jumping in, she stripped down in seconds. She wanted action and was anxious to get it on. The only things she wore were a button-down blouse, Bermuda shorts, and sandals – no underwear. Don gazed at this vision that was just put in front of him.

She said, "Well, what do you think?"

Don seemed to have lost his power of speech, with his mouth agape. He whispered, "They're beautiful, Baby! Can I have a taste?"

He could see her nipples were fully extended. She was heaving her hips slowly in a hypnotic, rhythmic motion. Don reach down, cupping a breast. He took her nipple, gently running his tongue over it and sucking. Her fluids began to flow with flavor that made his erection even harder.

He thought, *She must have gotten knocked up or something.*

She reached down, unbuckling his belt, and slid Don's jeans and underwear down to the floor.

Cupping his testicles in her hand, she then slid up and took hold of his prick, stroking him slowly. She massaged his knob with her thumb. Don was confused, not knowing whether to come or to hold. He chose to hold.

He reached down to her shaved, wet lips that opened so easily when he pushed on them gently with his middle finger. She whispered, "Wait ... Wait!"

Reaching into the pocket of the door, she took out a plastic bottle of Hershey's Chocolate Syrup. She covered her breasts with the sweet flowing liquid of the Aztec gods. "Okay ... now come and eat your candy!"

Then another chocolate memory popped into his head as Don drifted to his childhood when his father would make ice cream sundaes with homemade pure vanilla bean ice cream, hot chocolate sauce, marshmallow, and nuts. This treat was reserved for dessert after Sunday dinner. George, Don's father, would start making it as soon as they got home from church. Mixing the ingredients, he placed them in the ice cream maker to cool down. Flipping the switch, little Donny was mesmerized by the metamorphoses. His father was gone now, and he'd been alone since his death. Don shook his head with anger. Snapping out of his trance, he finished the chocolate bar and prepared to do the deed he had come here to do. He flicked the wrapper onto the grass as if it were one of his cigarette butts.

He slipped a black mask over his head that went down to his shoulders. "Don't forget the handcuffs," he mumbled to himself as he slid them under his belt in the middle of his back.

At the door, his hand automatically reached for the bell, stopping just before he touched the button. *Come on. Slow down. Don't make any stupid mistakes!*

Gently, he opened the screen door. His right hand tried the doorknob. To his surprise, it turned smooth as a greased pig. He pushed it open, quietly inhaling the aromas in Julie's home. Don could smell the burnt blood from the steak she'd fried hours earlier.

Sneaking quietly, he entered the kitchen. The grease-spattered cast iron pan still sat on the stove.

He ran his tongue over his lower lip as he opened the refrigerator; the bulb gave just enough light for him to find leftovers from her steak, potato, and green bean dinner. He picked up the cold steak and bit down hard, savoring the meat she had put away for later. *It's not like she'll be needing this for lunch tomorrow*, he smirked. He took two fingers and scooped up a mouthful of mashed potatoes, then grabbed an open bottle of milk and emptied it in four gulps.

Don walked over to her Lazy Boy recliner, kicked back quietly, looked around at her books, and fantasized Julie was bringing him a cold beer. Looking up to the ceiling, he visualized her lips coming down to greet his face with open kisses to his mouth, cheek, nose, and forehead. He thought, *Good God, you can't get any better than that!*

Getting up from the chair, he crept down the hallway. Passing the bathroom, he felt the humidity from the shower

Julie had taken before retiring. A digital clock sat on the counter, sending out an eerie red glow that flickered off the mirror. He saw a wet towel hanging on the shower door and moved closer.

He nestled his nose into the towel, taking in the clean, fresh smell of rose-perfumed soap. Closing his eyes, Don leaned forward and felt the tightening in his stomach muscles as he arched his pelvis into the imaginary figure beneath him.

From the other room came a loud snort. He jumped slightly, realizing where he was. He thought, *You got to be kidding, she snores? Oh well, I guess love is a give and take situation!*

But it was Don who was about to do the taking. A moment later, he crept over the threshold into her bedroom. There Julie lay, flat on her back. Her hands were on either side of her head, outlining her features with palms up. She breathed heavily. All of a sudden, she stopped breathing for the longest time. Don bent over her with curiosity as she gasped for breath, turning her body away from him, rolling onto her left side. He imagined she would be naked, but to his surprise, she was wearing a white cotton top with miniature blue rocking horses and a pair of blue silk panties with a red heart, front and center. He could see her clearly, the nightlight giving a luminous aura to the room. He had finally fulfilled his deepest desire: to see Julie in bed and to be with her.

Don stood for the longest time, looking at her body and thinking of all the perverted ways he would take pleasure from it. Creeping closer, he knelt down next to the back of Julie's head, smelling her hair. The rose-perfumed soap filled the air. *Come, my love, it's time to go.*

Being right handed, he did a cross draw from the left hip, reaching for the double-bladed Puma hunting knife in the sheath. He then slid his left hand under the left side of Julie's neck, taking care not to move the pillow as he went, and quickly brought his hand around her left jaw and over her mouth before she could come completely out of her slumber.

He snapped her head back against his chest with such an adrenaline rush force it put her in total shock. Julie lay there wide-eyed with terror, unable to move. A flash of light gleamed off the blade as he placed it to her neck. She felt the cold steel resting on her skin as her carotid artery pulsated against the knife. "Don't move a muscle. I don't wanna' hurt you. Do you understand?"

The only thing Julie could do was sob a deep, soft cry way down in her throat.

"Now I want you to slide out of the bed, kneeling with your face down, you got it?"

Julie replied with a low whine and moved very slowly onto the floor. Don mounted her back and grabbed a fist full of her hair. Pulling her head back, he looked into her closed eyes. "Open your fuckin' eyes ... bitch."

She submitted as she looked into a Black Death mask greeting her fears. Her tears washed over the rubber-covered hand still clamping her mouth closed.

"Julie, do everything I tell you. Don't make a sound, or I will shove this fuckin' knife clean through you. You understand?" She nodded her head in compliance.

A thought flashed through Julie's mind like a bolt of lightning. *He knows my name*!

Remembering he'd heard wild horses remain calm when blindfolded, he released his grip on her mouth, reached over, and grabbed her pillow. Removing the case, he slipped it roughly over her head.

"Okay," Don whispered in a low, raspy voice, "Now I want you to stand up, and do it slowly. I don't want you to speak unless I say you can, you hear?"

Julie nodded once more. Pulling her hair, he stood her up, spun her around, and nudged her toward the open doorway. Julie's feet made a plopping sound as she was off balance with her head pulled back and her hands out, feeling her way down the dark hallway.

Don found this a complete turn-on. He had a full erection, and he kept bumping it into her as he guided her into the kitchen. He whispered into her ear, "Oh, you've got such a sweet ass!"

"Okay! Julie, I'm gonna' let go of the pillowcase for a second. Keep still, you hear?"

Once again, she grunted in compliance.

Tonight would be the first of hundreds of times she would comply. Placing the knife on the counter, he reached into his jacket pocket and removed the bottle of chloroform.

Julie smelled the pungent odor as he poured a generous amount onto a rag. She asked, shaken, "What's that?"

"I told you to shut the fuck up!" Don grabbed the pillowcase, tightening the material against her face. With one swift movement, he shoved the cloth over her nose and mouth. Letting go of her hair, he placed his left hand on her forehead and pulled back with all of his strength. Julie struggled, clawing and digging her nails into his gloved hands to no avail before dizziness took over. She lost consciousness, and then fell to the floor with a thud.

This whole control thing is such a turn-on! Don looked down at Julie's comatose body and visualized her begging to be fucked hard. He whispered, "Can't touch this. You bitch, you can't touch it."

He kept singing the song repeatedly while masturbating until he came all over her. Then grabbing her by her hands, he pulled her headfirst out the back door. He slid her on a small kitchen rug that helped with dragging her dead weight.

When he got her out on the back porch, he propped her up against the wall. Moving the wheelbarrow up tight to the steps, he straddled her. Reaching under her arms, he gave her a bear hug, and at the same time, he lifted her with a grunt. One quick turn, and she was above the open pit of the wheelbarrow.

He tried to let her down gently, but her 200-plus-pound weight was too much for him. Julie slipped out of his hands, landing with a crash and hitting her head on the rim of the wheelbarrow with a loud crack.

Looking down at her body, Don chuckled inside, *Well, if you weren't out before, you are now!*

He placed the chloroform cloth over her nose and mouth just as a precautionary move to make sure she did stay down. Julie was a sorry sight with a lump on the back of her head, her feet protruding out the front of the wheelbarrow, a pillowcase over her head, and dressed in clothes no one was supposed to see.

Just then, he heard one of her neighbor's talking loudly. "God damn mutts, Mabel, you think people would keep their dogs on a chain. I know there's gonna' be a mess to clean up in the mornin'!"

Don jumped into the tall bushes next to the driveway, hiding just in case the neighbor came out to look for what he thought was a dog. A few minutes passed before the neighbor's lights finally went out. Putting the kitchen rug over Julie's comatose body, he laughed to himself. *She reminds me of Oliver Hardy. All she needs is a mustache and bowler hat.*

Three

Lost and Found

One day in late winter, about two months before he snatched Julie, Don had drank all his booze so he went out to refill the cupboard. He stopped by Kelly's Liquor Store to restock his supply with a half-gallon of Southern Comfort and a case of Giant Imperial Quarts. He'd been drinking these brands of liquor since he was a kid. Since he was at the store stocking up on what he considered essentials, he picked up a fresh carton of Camels, too.

He stood at the front counter waiting for his change when he saw a rather large woman sashay past the front door of the liquor store. Don acted like a big tomcat that smelled an amorous kitty cat in heat. He could not take his eyes off of her. *Could that be Julie? Certainly looks like her!*

He did a double take and almost forgot to collect his change for the "C" note he had handed the clerk. He bolted out of the store just in time to see her going into the Blue Bag Grocery next door. Hurriedly, he made his way to his car to stash his booze. He reached up and pulled the trunk lid down with a slam as he glanced back to the store. He ran toward the entrance and grabbed a grocery cart on the way through the sliding glass doors.

In no time, he caught up to her. Don felt the excitement; his heart raced with amorous desire. He went up one aisle and down the next, following her all of the way. He tried to get closer to her. His cart overflowed as he grabbed almost every item he passed, pretending to shop.

If he could just talk to her, he could make sure it was really Julie. Beads of perspiration covered his forehead as his anxiety built; finally, he made his move. With a hop-skip-jump, he bumped into her as if she were a hockey player he was going to check on the ice. She turned, and their eyes met. Don was face to face not a foot away from her.

Julie's eyes opened wide, "Oh, why don't you watch where you're goin'?" With that, she put her hand on her hip, "That hurts!"

"Oh, I am so sorry ... I ... I didn't see you. Please forgive me!"

"Yeah, yeah, but be more careful, will ya'?"

Don then made a quizzical face, "Julie, is that you?"

"Do I know you? Who are you?" She didn't let on he'd gotten her name right, but this made her uneasy.

"Don't you remember me? From grade school ... remember fourth grade?"

"Fourth grade, are you kiddin'?" Julie scowled at him with disdain, "No! Leave me alone, you jerk!" Then she pushed her cart forward, around the corner to the next aisle, and out of his life.

Don stood there dumbstruck and feeling lost in the spice aisle between the Spanish and Italian herbs. He stood there for the longest time, not believing what had happened. The love of his life simply walked away from him after all these years. He felt totally abandoned once again.

The other person who had abandoned him was his mother. That foul memory leapt into his mind, and it stung even now when he remembered how she had caused him even more pain when she remarried. She seemed to turn her back on him, paying less and less attention to him after his father's death. Before he fully understood what had happened to his father, he found himself in boarding school hardly ever seeing his mother. When he did, she felt like a stranger.

Leaving the overflowing grocery cart where it stood, he headed for the exit door. Humiliated and humbled, he immediately pulled out a smoke and lit up, mumbling to himself all the way to his car. He sat there in a daze, staring at the front door of the store, with memories overwhelming him. He could still clearly see every petal of the embroidered sunflowers on the pink dress Julie wore the first day of kindergarten, the first day he had ever seen her. She was heavier than the other children were, but she had a sweet face, long blond hair, and beautiful large blue eyes. That's what he'd fallen in love with; those eyes and that face had made little Donny sick with an emotion he couldn't understand ... puppy love.

Donny considered himself Julie's best friend. He shared his miniature cars and toy soldiers with her in the sand box, and he delighted when she asked him to help her dress her dolls up in outfits; he didn't care what the other boys thought. They'd play together from the time their mothers dropped them off until the day was over.

Then his devastation at losing Julie when he was ten years old, when his mother sent him away after his father's death, flowed over him as if it had all happened yesterday. Donny didn't get the chance to say goodbye to Julie when his father died. One day he was there in school, and the next day he was gone. Donny's mother sent him off to a boarding school while she languished in depression for months, lying in bed after her husband's sudden death. Don lost three significant people at once, and the loss changed him forever. For reasons he never comprehended, of the three, somehow losing Julie felt like the most crushing blow, defying all logic.

Reliving the pain, he sat and chain-smoked almost a full pack waiting for her to come out so he could just see her one more time. Maybe she would remember him now. After all, she'd had some time in the store to think about this stranger. It took forever, but finally she came out of the grocery.

Don said aloud, as if she could actually hear him, "Julie, how could you trash me like that? I thought you were my friend. I just can't believe it! After all of these years, you treat me like this?"

Julie pushed the grocery cart across the parking lot, right in Don's direction. She was coming his way!

He thought, W*hat should I do now?* His first impulse was to approach her again to plead forgiveness for his fumbling ways. Don considered what he might say to smooth things over. *Hi Julie, I thought that I could say hello once more after my awkward approach. You know, when I saw you, I was just so blown away because I remembered what fun we had in grammar school.*

Instead, he slumped down in the car seat, trying to hide. She was parked in the next row and couldn't have been thirty feet away. Julie stopped and looked around as if she were scanning the parking lot for some deranged person who might be stalking her. Don hid with only his forehead and eyes showing above the dash, looking like Kilroy, the cartoon character the U.S. troops drew all over Europe during the Second World War. She never even spotted him hiding in that position. When she felt safe, she loaded her groceries into the trunk of her car and immediately got into the driver's seat, slamming the door.

Lead-foot Lilly booted the gas, and Don had a big problem trying to keep up with her flashy but older BMW. She turned off Massachusetts Avenue onto Mohawk Street and pulled into the driveway all the way to the backdoor. Don passed the house slowly. He saw the numbers on the mailbox: 69 Mohawk Street.

Don was mad – real mad. He'd known other women before, and none had ever treated him as crude as this. "Okay, Julie Booker, you have it your way for now, but I'll be back, you bitch! You'll see, I'll be back!"

Four

Gentleman Caller

Don drove past Julie's home every night after their chance encounter. He was tempted to stop, knock on the door, and maybe even attempt to introduce himself again. Three weeks later, he stopped at eleven o'clock at night after circling the block eight times. He parked his car down the street.

Looking around, he quickly made his way to her front door. Stepping onto the threshold, he peeked into the hallway and saw a nightlight on a small table. After waiting for a few minutes, trying to get up the gumption to knock, he went around to the right side of the house where he noticed a light shining through the window. Approaching carefully, he saw Julie lying down in bed with a book propped up on her knees.

Yeah, he thought, *that makes sense. She loved books from before we even learned how to read 'em. She was always the first to be able to read the tough new stuff. When the teacher had her read the stories to the whole class, it was magic ... she made it magic. All the kids would sit around her when she read, and they wanted to be her best friend, too. They were trying to horn in on what was mine even then!*

Don watched her and fantasized what he would do if he were next to her in bed. He puckered his lips and flicked his tongue as if he were a snake, in and out, imagining he was licking between her legs. His emotions got the best of him, as he was touching and stroking himself quickly. Unconsciously Don must have moaned, for at that very crucial moment in his masturbation, Julie put the book down. She peered out into the darkness of the night, right into his eyes. He could see into her deep baby blues, but all she could see was the blackness of the night.

He imagined her sharing his feelings of ecstasy. It was a real turn on for him. Coupled with his excitement from the possibility of getting caught, every muscle in his body tightened and his sperm spewed out onto the ground.

"Is someone there?" She squinted, trying to see. This tempted Don to call out to her as if he were coming to serenade her. But he thought better for a moment as he placed his now limp dick into his pants and zipped up his fly, deciding to beat a hasty retreat and wait for a more opportune time.

Don hopped into his car and drove down the street. Pulling over to the side of the road, he reached into the glove box for the pint of Southern Comfort he always kept there. As he gulped the sweet whiskey, it burned all the way down to his gut. Reflecting, Don thought about how he usually felt cool as a cucumber. It surprised and upset him that he felt bothered.

"I guess I feel this way because this was special, because it was Julie." He lit up a smoke and wheeled back onto the road.

Don was not far from home, but he drove slowly and nursed the bottle all the way. He pulled into his driveway and misjudged the distance from the garage because of the booze. His front right bumper ripped the garage door off its hinges, knocking it to the ground. Don let out a long groan. "Ahhhhh! Oh no!"

He turned off the engine and sat there for a few minutes in a stupor. "Shit, I must be fuckin' drunk! Ohhhhhh ... I don't feel so good."

Don curled up into a fetal position and fell into a deep slumber on the front seat. Next thing he knew the sun was shining in his face, waking him up. He sat there in a daze, trying to remember why he was sleeping in the car. Don rubbed his head. *What the fuck happened last night? I can't remember.*

Slowly his memory came back, "Oh yeah!" He smiled. Gazing out the window at the grass as if in a fog, he said, "God damn it the fuckin' grass is too high again."

Five

Preparation for the Snatch

Lying in bed staring at the ceiling, Don thought, *How am I gonna' snatch her? It's not gonna' be easy. Julie must be at least two hundred pounds of loveliness or damn close to it ... she might kick my ass and give me a good beating. She could be one tough broad if this ain't done just right. Oh man, she's gonna' be my beauty ... you wait and see. It'll take planning; you can't just go ahead and snatch someone. I gotta' make an inventory list of all the good things I gotta' get. Handcuffs are out of the question. They wouldn't reach from one wrist to the other behind her back. Hmmm ... Maybe three linked together would work.*

I'll keep her in the basement, in the old coal room. It wouldn't take much to build a cell. The door could be made of welded bars, just like they got in them prison movies. I'll make it comfortable and cozy ... she'll love it down there!

With much pondering and imagination, it all came to light. "*Chloroform ... yes, chloroform ... that'll do the trick! I can see it all. I'll sneak up to the back door and knock; when she opens the door, I'll just shove the chloroform rag over her mouth and nose 'til she conks out. Hmmm ... I'll have to protect myself by wearing plastic gloves – no fingerprints, no chemicals.*

Yeah, and I'll wear a ski mask, too! Just in case things don't go accordin' to Hoyle. Well, I can see it all now. She's on the floor and knocked out cold ... wait ... how the hell am I gonna' move her? Don pondered for a moment. "How 'bout a wheelbarrow?" he answered himself out loud. "Of course, that's the answer!"

Don climbed into the cab of his Toyota pickup truck that he bought last week from Jerry's Pre-owned Car Lot. He chiseled the guy down from $3,999 to $1,500, although he had to buy it "AS IS" with no guarantee or warranty with the purchase. *You never know,* he'd thought, *I may need a truck to haul her ass back to my place.*

Home Depot was just five miles away with everything he needed for a little felonious home improvement project. It was raining cats and dogs; he had a difficult time seeing the road clearly. While approaching the intersection of Main Street and Elm, he inadvertently went over the white line because of the poor visibility, causing the Gestapo police traffic camera to take his photo for a red light violation. "Welcome to 2010 – all things have come to pass per George Orwell! What more will this government do to raise taxes?" he cursed as he flicked a butt out the window at the camera.

Don pulled into the empty parking lot. The engine was running a little rough. *Probably needs a tune up*, he noted mentally and then gunned the engine, turning the key off.

"Good evening, Sir, welcome to Home Depot, may I be of help?" Don was still a good distance from the greeter and didn't say anything until he got closer.

He thought to himself, *Son of a bitch, he just wants to make me feel at ease so he can screw me. This place has been a rip off since they knocked out the competition. I remember old man Abraham Jacobs' hardware store, passed down from father to son. Abraham bein' the fifth generation of Jacobs' to run the store; it had been here since the Civil War. He had so much old stuff. Stuff so old you couldn't even tell what it was used for.*

I remember findin' an antique apple peeler buried under a pile of rusty roofing nails. It was so easy to use – just stick an apple on the end of the fork and turn the crank. In five seconds, you'd have a cleaned apple ready for a pie. He died of a broken heart when all of his friends went to the new fuckin' Home Depot.

Walking into the brightly lit store, Don approached the clerk, who seemed to be screwing off and got into the man's face, violating his space. "I need a good, high-quality commercial wheelbarrow – double front wheels."

The clerk stepped back one pace. "Yes, Sir, three aisles down on your left, and go to the back of the store."

"Thanks. Where's the chloroform?"

"Nah, we don't carry that! You'll have to go to a chemical supply house."

"Thanks," he grunted as he grabbed a shopping cart. Don thought to himself, *I just love the smell of a hardware store. Look at all those cool gadgets.*

In the back of the store, he found the perfect commercial wheelbarrow. "There's plenty of room for her!"

He quickly glanced around to see if anyone had heard him thinking aloud. He left the shopping cart there and continued to make his rounds using his newly acquired super-duper double-wheeled wheelbarrow to tote everything he needed. Pulling the shopping list from his pocket, he read over it again to be sure he hadn't forgotten anything:

1. One nylon rope – twenty foot long and smooth as silk.
2. A six-foot stepladder.
3. Three boxes of ten-penny nails.
4. Twenty two-by-fours, eight foot tall.
5. Forty rebar rods, for making the cell bars.
6. One new flush toilet, to be fitted onto the old sewer pipe in the corner of the basement.
7. A set of construction lights with twenty bulbs that will activate just by plugging into a wall socket that has a light switch.
8. One small college-style refrigerator.
9. Ten cases of bottled water – 32 ounces each.
10. Rubber gloves.
11. Two two-by-eights, twelve foot long.
12. A new mailbox with post, to install curbside to keep the postman off the porch and out of earshot of the house, just in case she starts screaming.

"Let's see, at home I already got some hammers, a hand saw, table saw, levels, square, and an extra-heavy-duty, thick extension cord. Well, that's all that I can think of for now."

As Don walked up to the checkout station, he checked out the cashier. She was a woman who obviously did not belong in a Home Depot, never mind working in such a place. Well dressed, she wore a multi-colored, short-sleeved silk shirt with matching bandana. Covering her rather shapely legs, she wore expensive, tailored Bermuda shorts. All of this was topped off with a bright orange apron with "Home Depot" in white letters across her chest. She was over sixty, tanned, and damn good looking for her age. He thought, *Good legs for an old broad.*

"Hi," she said with a smile as if she was welcoming an old friend, "and did we find everything we were looking for?"

She made Don feel very uncomfortable. S*he acts like my mother or my fourth grade teacher at my grammar school, Ms. Corcoran.*

"Yeah ... yeah, thanks."

The cashier reached over the counter with the electric scanner to read the bar codes. He saw the Rolex watch on her wrist. Watching to see if it was sweeping or ticking, he saw it was sweeping. She also had expensive rings with large diamonds on her wedding finger.

"Wow, nice taste ... I really like your rings."

"Why, thank you, young man. I can see you have good taste."

"Why are you working here? You don't belong here!"

She lowered her eyes, her face saddened, and she bit her lower lip. "Things change, don't they? My Herb, he passed suddenly last month. He handled everything for me. He was the love of my life and my soul mate. Now I must try to carry on without him, so here I am, working at The Home Depot. It's so hard to find a job when you've never worked outside the house. I am sixty five, and all I ever had to do was be a loving wife to a wonderful man." She smiled and said, "Herb was fifteen years older than me. He would say, 'Dorothy, I love showing you off!'"

Changing the subject back to business, she said, "Well, it looks as if we are adding onto our house, or are you a contractor?"

"Ahhhhh ... yeah, yeah ... ahhhhh ... I'm building a new recreation room in my basement for the love of my life."

"Oh, that is so nice. She will be so happy. Will it be a surprise for her?"

Don's eyes lit up, and a big smile came to his face. He chuckled, "We'll be getting married ... we're going to have a family. We're going to have a big family, maybe four or five kids. Oh, we're going to be so happy!"

"I am sure you will be. You are such a nice young man. God will be good to you."

As Don turned and walked away, he told her, "Thank you, Ma'am, you're so kind. You have a good night."

Don then whispered to himself, "Yeah, she talks just the way my mom did, the way she used to be ... before Dad died in the car wreck and she married that fuckin' asshole only a year later."

Meeting this fine lady working as a clerk brought back too many bittersweet remembrances of Don's childhood and the Mom that he used to have. He missed the motherly warmth and tender touch only she could give. It also brought back images of his stepfather berating him to stop practicing his boxing on his makeshift punching bag and go out to mow the enormous lawn at his mansion. Shaking off his melancholy with anger, he yelled in the cab of his truck, "Fuck it – fuck her – I'm gonna' get me Julie to give me some lovin' now."

Six

Burger Delight

Don loaded the materials into the back of the pickup and used the long rope to tie down everything securely. Flipping on the radio, he heard Bob "The Burger Man" Swartz singing the ad jingle for Burger Delight.

"Burger Delight is the place to go for food that is always right,

For food that's always right,

For food that's always right!

Burger Delight is the place to go for food that is always right!"

"Woo, woo," tooted a foghorn in the background.

"That's right, boys and girls! Head down to Burger Delight. It's located right on Mass. Ave. at the Cambridge Line. You tell 'em that I sent you."

"Woo, Woo!"

Well, that was enough to start the juices flowing in Don's mouth. "Oh yeah, man, a big fat Delight Burger! That's just what the doctor ordered."

He slammed his truck into first gear. With a squeal, burning a cloud of rubber, he pulled out of the Home Depot parking lot and headed for the Cambridge Line. He wheeled into the line of traffic turning into the burger joint.

"This place hasn't changed since I was in high school," he said, looking around. "I remember when six of us pitched in and bought an old hearse with the casket wheels still in the back. It still gives me the creeps when I think of it. Everybody knew that it was our rolling bar on rubber. The broads used to love it, too, with the mattress for lovin'. We had to take up three parking spaces in the lot with that thing."

He remembered he used to watch the cars go round all night long until they scored with some skirts. He saw the same thing going on now with hot rods parked in the back of the lot lined up so they could observe and try to pick up girls who were also on the prowl. A waitress with shoulder-length bleach blond hair and a petite body came rolling over to take Don's order. She wore a short yellow skirt with a skimpy red blouse emblazoned with "B. D." on the front.

"Hey Sweetie, what'll y'all have?" she drawled with a distinctly southern accent.

Don raised his right eyebrow, "I'll have you, Sweetie."

"Not on your life!" she grinned. "Hell would freeze over first!"

Don flushed red with embarrassment, "Delight Burger, fries, and a large Coke."

She skated away quickly. The skates made her appear taller than her five foot five frame. He watched her skirt flip to-and-fro as she disappeared around the side of the building and into the restaurant.

Opening a new pack of Camels, he carefully ripped the tinfoil to leave a flap to fold back so he could keep the other butts fresh and in the pack. The smoke wafted up as he watched the slew of cars and the cast of characters that continually drove by. Half an hour later, she came back with a big smile and a tray she hung on the outside of the truck door.

"Sorry it took so long, but they're backed up in the kitchen." Don paid for the food and gave her an extra five dollars as a tip.

"Oh ... that's too much."

"No, no, you deserve it for all the crap you take all night long. Sorry ... about before … "Don looked at her name badge, "JoJo. So is that really your name?"

She looked down at the badge, "Yeah, it is."

He said, "Cute name!"

She smiled, "Thanks. Well, got to go."

"Wait, wait, what's the rush?"

"I got to go! What would my boyfriend say?"

"What would he say about what?"

JoJo paused for a moment, "What's your name, Sugah?"

Don paused as if he forgot his own name. "Um, Donald ... it's Don!"

She smiled, "Come back and see me again, y'all hear?" As she skated away, she gave him a backhanded wave.

Don murmured as if he had just tasted a sweet, Southern peach pie. "Mummm." Out of earshot of the Southern belle, he said with confidence, "You know, I will be coming back, Sugah."

Funny thing is she knows what I'm thinking. A chill ran up his right shoulder as he imagined her sitting nude in his lap.

Seven

Chloroform

While driving home, Don talked to himself, reminiscing about high school. *"Funny thing, most people forget the bad times in their teens. You know, when it was so lonely you thought you would die from the hurt? You had no friends to stick up for you. Ha, that's when I learned to kick ass. No one fucked with me then! I remember Joan in chemistry class. She would always get pissed when I'd mix all different shit in the beaker and watch it boil over like a volcano. Wait a minute ... chemistry class ... I know where I can get some chloroform! There's plenty up in the lab at the high school. We had to use it to knock out frogs and mice in biology lab class."*

He drove straight down to Ike Eisenhower Memorial High School, spinning around the corner of the field and track house into the dark shadows. He stopped right under the fire escape ladder coming down from the roof of the main building. Grabbing a crowbar from the toolbox under the seat, he scrambled onto the cab of his truck, enabling him to reach the ladder.

Once on the roof, he headed for the bulkhead. The ballast stones made a racket as his feet shuffled across the roof.

Damn it – these stones are so fuckin' noisy. Good thing no one's around.

Putting his crowbar into the crack of the bulkhead door, it popped open as if it were never locked. He went down one flight to the second floor and turned left. *The fifth door on the right should be the lab*, he recalled.

He had no problem walking in the semi-darkness; red exit signs lit the inside of the school. The smell of the hallway brought back so many memories. Don felt like it was only yesterday. Lab class had been a joke for him; he had aced it.

Reaching for the doorknob, Don attempted to turn it. *Damn it ... it's locked!* There was no space to wedge the crowbar into the crack. Noticing the glass pane in the upper half of the door, he tapped the glass with the jimmy bar. It dropped onto the classroom floor with a loud crash. Reaching inside, he turned the handle, unlocking the door.

The chloroform bottle was locked in the glass cabinets; they opened easily with the crowbar. Even in the gloom, Don had no trouble identifying the contents of the large, dark brown bottle marked in bold red letters one inch high with a skull and crossbones beneath the word: CHLOROFORM.

Taking a stroll for old time's sake, he went into the teachers' lounge. Just inside the door stood a cigarette machine set up by one of the local mob guys. Once again, Don's trusty crowbar came into play. Placing the blade on the hinge at the side of the machine, he pushed down with all of his weight. The hinge bent, and with one last effort, Don heard a loud pop.

The door swung open, displaying the multi-colors of hundreds of cigarette packages bearing the tax stamp of

North Carolina. These were smuggled in small vans from the South to evade the sales tax of "Taxachusetts." The vender passed the savings onto the smoking teachers to avoid having someone blow the whistle on him. If someone did, he would simply play "Mickey the Dunce."

"Hey, I didn't know my teachers smoked bootlegs; I buy all my butts legit."

Don also checked the change box, looking inside. He knew venders often hid money in the machines, using the box as a bank. Don counted the bills and then whispered, "Bin-go-o-o, I hit the jackpot! Twenty-two hundred bucks ... not bad." Sliding the cash into the right rear pocket of his dungarees, he smiled and raised his eyebrows.

Looking around, Don found an industrial-size box of paper towels in the closet; he emptied the rolls out onto the floor. Next, he unlatched the shelf that held his smokes for the next year. The shelf swung open and packs of cigarettes rained down onto the floor with a soft patter-patter-patter.

Placing the jug of chloroform in the middle of the box, he used the cigarettes as cushions. Don spied a roll of the paper towels. Wiping off all surfaces he may have touched, he smiled as he thought to himself, *No fingerprints – no evidence.*

Don slipped back up onto the roof. He experienced the same noisy clattering with each step. The smooth, round stones moved as he advanced to the fire escape ladder. Peering down to the truck below, he whispered, "Shit – that's a long fuckin' drop."

His inner voice told him it would be foolish to attempt the descent holding the large box with one arm and his life with the other. He removed the bottle from the box and squeezed it into the large leg pocket on his right side – it just fit.

Then, holding the large box of cigarettes by two fingers on each side, he let go as if he were a bombardier. It sailed like it was being held by invisible hands all the way to the ground. On impact, it landed upright with a thud. Don smiled with satisfaction as he once again overcame adversity. Holding onto the ladder, he did not look down as he eased himself ever so carefully until he felt the grass underfoot.

He turned the key; the motor caught, purring softly. Don turned the corner of the building without switching on the headlights. He gasped as he saw a police cruiser parked under an old maple tree.

"Oh fuck!" His heart raced as he realized that he was going to be busted for breaking and entering. Without touching the gas, the truck glided across the grass like a phantom, disappearing from view. The cop was sleeping, or as it was called by the fuzz, "going under."

"That fucker was so sound asleep that he never knew that I was there."

He laughed all the way down the road, releasing the adrenaline and nervous tension that had built up in his body. Needless to say, he did not break the speed limit. "Can you imagine, comin' around a corner and see a fuckin' cruiser sittin' in the shadows after just doin' a B and E. That blew my fuckin' mind."

Don felt beat. He'd had a hard night of shopping for supplies and had flirted with JoJo half the evening as well. Getting home late, he slept until eight the next evening. He did not get up right away but lay in bed with his eyes closed. It seemed like hours passed. All he could think about was how life sucked.

It's not fair ... I'm all alone and lonesome. I wish things would change! Everyone I've ever known has someone, but not me.

His solitary existence would change soon, although perhaps not for the better. He was about to take Julie against her will. Having her body would not be the same as having her heart and mind, but Don didn't realize it at the time. It was as if he was back living in a cave using a club to enforce his own law.

Eight

Robin

Grabbing his truck keys, Don drove down the dark streets in the middle of the night. This was the only thing he could do to relieve the unbearable anxiety when he experienced an attack. Breathing the fresh air, with all different odors wafting from the blooms of the spring night, put him at ease. He passed the dimly lit streetlights one after the other as he went from town to town until he arrived at Revere Beach.

Parking at the curb, he stepped onto the sand. The smell blowing in from the sea was different here, tinged with the damp, dank, musty smell of low tide caused by decomposing seaweed that had built up with the incoming tides. Mixed in was the stench of the overflowing trash barrels waiting to be emptied at the crack of dawn by city workers.

The full moon hung low in the night sky, shining over the bay with such brilliance and detail Don could almost touch it. Being here eased his soul; it brought back memories of his childhood, when he came here with his mom and dad.

When he was a kid, an amusement park had stretched for miles in an arc from the fishing pier all the way to the Nahant Bridge. Thoughts of the cotton candy were so real and sweet they made his mouth water. He recalled the toys, prizes, and games of chance, as well as the barkers who gave the illusion that one could win the games.

George and Mary had purchased a home on the bay in Gloucester, on the Upper North Shore, only 30 miles up from Revere Beach and the amusement park. On a clear day, they could see Maine in the distance. Like most professionals, George's work consumed his life, but he took solace in the fact he could spend most weekends alone up on the North Shore, just he and Mary and their son Donald.

Little Donny was the symbol of their marriage, their treasured wedding baby conceived of perfect, joyful love on the night of their honeymoon. George had always wanted a family to provide for and this was the core of his being. Although he spent a great deal of time away supporting them by working in Boston, he tried to make up for it by showering them with all the privileges and indulgences his success could buy. Donny loved this amusement park, so his Dad brought the family here many summer weekends. Mary had everything she wanted, also. They all relaxed at the boat club, the spa, the country club, and lived in the lap of luxury. They seemed to live an enchanted life, until the insane work hours claimed George's life on his drive home one blustery night.

Don stood there, reminiscing the times at the beach, and recalled the delicious seafood he used to eat as a kid. Suddenly, he realized this particular memory had been prompted by mouthwatering aromas of fried clams and onion rings drifting in from the restaurant across the street. The little place had opened its doors in the midst of the roaring twenties and had been in operation ever since. Don's stomach rumbled, as he had not eaten since he had met JoJo at Burger Delight. All of a sudden, his melancholia disappeared as he quickened his pace, striding from the beach to the counter of the take-out bar across the street.

The cashier had a cigarette smoldering in an ashtray next to the register. The man asked, "What'll ya' have, Palie?"

"I'll have a clam plate with extra clams, fries, plus a Coke."

The cashier leaned toward the microphone, "One extra clam with fries." Picking up his cigarette and taking a long drag as he spoke, the smoke exhausted from his mouth and nostrils at the same time. He asked, "Hey Palie, ya' wanna' extra-large drink for a quartah' more? Ya' can't beat the price anywhere on the beach."

"Sure ... sure." As Don turned, he saw a vision of loveliness who wore red, high-heeled platform shoes with sparkling sequins that glittered as she approached. Don caught his breath with a soft whistle.

She smiled as she lifted her shoulders and moved only as a woman who was also smitten could, or should, move. She appeared longer-legged because of the shoes. Don thought to himself, *Man, look at those legs. They go all the way up to her ass.* An involuntary spasm made his shoulders shudder like a little puppy.

It did not hinder her movements to have old cut-off dungarees that had more holes than material. They clung to her hips; she let them hang down to stop just under her pierced belly button. Don imagined she must be clean-shaven. She was firm, tanned, and looking good in a black corset top.

An old wives' tale says women who have long hair are fertile, love to love, and are easy to approach. Her hair hung six inches below her waist, looked shiny black as coal, and smelled fresh as sunshine even though it was past midnight.

Don looked her right in the eyes, nodded his head, and smiled, "You came to the right place at the right time!"

"Oh, really … why do you say that?"

"That's because the dinner is on me. That is ... as long as we dine together."

"You're so sweet and kind! Thank you ... sure ... I would love that."

He was leaning on the counter but extended his hand, "Hi, I'm Don."

"I'm Robin."

"Well, now that we've gotten over the first bump in the road, what will you have?"

Robin returned the compliment by staring back deeply into Don's eyes, "I'll have whatever you're going to have."

Don turned to the smoking cashier and said sarcastically, "Hey Palie, make that a double."

The cashier smiled out of the side of his mouth, still puffing on the butt with a steady stream of smoke going into his eyes that made them water. "Sure kid, no problem." He called into the microphone. "Harry – that last ordah', make it for two."

A high-pitched voice from back in the kitchen answered, "You got it."

"Hey Palie, that'll be twenty-four fifty, including tax."

Don reached into his pocket and pulled out the two grand of cash he took from the cigarette machine. He peeled off a hundred dollar bill and paid for the food. Don made sure Robin saw the roll was all hundreds, not just a couple of big bills wrapped around a wad of singles. He thought, *I don't want her thinking I'm just flashing a nigger roll.* As they started some small talk, they were surprised when their food order came up quickly.

Robin said, “Well, it just goes to show you how time flies when you’re having such a good time. Shall we go across the street to the bandstand? They have picnic tables there. We can watch the surf roll in.”

Don popped a very large Ipswich fried clam with a huge belly into his mouth and bit down. The rich, delicious flavor of the fresh clam, an acquired taste loved by people who grow up on seacoasts, filled his mouth, making him salivate even more. The mingled taste of salt mud flats, as well as the smell of low tide, and what the clam had eaten for its last meal, filled his mouth.

“Mummm, good! You know, this place has the best clams of anybody on the beach.”

“Yeah, I know. I just love to come here. It’s so earthy.”

“Robin, what brings you out this time of night?”

“I just got off work from The Club.”

“Oh, what do you do there? Work the bar?” Don knew better but decided to play it low key.

“No, I’m an exotic dancer four nights a week, and a full-time student at Boston University.”

“Wow, Boston University ... what’s your major?” Don thought to himself, *I wonder if this is just a bunch of bullshit.*

“Business major ... someday I want to run my own business.”

“Hey, that’s a cool thing to do. I can see you behind a big desk on the phone giving orders to others who work for you.” He continued, “Hey, I was thinking ... do you know of any openings at your night job? I could dance on ladies night!”

She smiled, “That’s kind of a different spin. Usually when I tell some guy I work at The Simplicity Club, he expects me to give him a blow job.” He could tell Robin was defensive because of all of the creeps she bumped into working at a strip joint.

"You know, this is an art. You have to be a good dancer to be able to survive and get top billing in show business. I've been dancing since I was five. Every time there was a school play, I was in it."

"Good for you! It's great to meet someone that wants to better themselves." Being a good listener, Don just leaned back and let Robin tell him all about herself.

"I'm from Lynn, Massachusetts, you know, next to Swampscott. I was kind of outgoing when I was growing up, even though my mom was on welfare and food stamps. That just made me determined to do better. I'm not going to be a second generation on welfare."

She told Don that many of the girls from work drove cars they rented from Rent-A-Wreck. She said, "By renting a junk box, stalkers can't find out where you live by running your license plate. Funny thing, the stalker is usually a cop with the city police department."

"Did anything bad ever happen to you?"

"No, not to me, but a good friend of mine was raped, murdered, and dumped in the Lynn salt marsh just last summer."

"Wow, she may just be the lucky one."

Robin stared at him in shock, offended and hurt by his statement. She thought, *What a jerk!* She said, "What do you mean by that?"

"Well, what if she was kidnapped and held in a basement as a sex slave?" Don started to get aroused. "What if ... what if he kept her until he made her to be just like he envisioned? He could even teach her how to please him. You know what I mean?"

Robin didn't say anything, as she was disgusted at what she was being told by this total stranger. Finally, she carefully put forth, "Don, it sounds like you like a little kinky sex, a little S&M. Do you? Do you like that?" she said with a chuckle.

"Well, maybe just a little, nothing too strong or out of the way. But I must be in control. I don't want someone to beat or humiliate me. I want to do the pissing; I don't want to be pissed on. I want to be the master. Get what I mean?"

Robin sensed a mark; she smiled a smile she knew would turn on any john she was working. Here was someone she could have some fun with and make him pay for it. She knew a place she could take him. She would give him all he wanted and deserved. She might even give him a little payback for his statements about her friend who was murdered. She would make sure he got more than he wanted out of their bargain.

It was strange; these johns always came back for more even though they swore once was enough. Robin considered herself addictive to anyone who had sex with her. She knew how to please.

"Don, why don't you come with me, and we could spend some quality time together."

"I can't make it tonight. But give me your phone number, and I'll give you a call."

"I can't give you my number! But you can give me yours. I'll call you on my next night off."

He quickly scribbled his number on the back of the clam shack receipt. They French kissed for the longest time, touching and groping. Don reached through the rips of her shorts to grab both her ass cheeks. He put pressure on her anus by rotating each cheek against the other. He knew this was a turn-on for a girl that likes the "Hershey Road," and given what she chose to reveal with her attire, he had a hunch it might be her thing. Don could not believe that she kept having orgasms one after another. He thought, *I've got to be good, or she's just faking it.*

Finally, out of breath, she gasped, "Thanks for dinner. I got to go."

He released her and she flipped her hip in a bump-and-grind mode as if she were still on stage while she walked to her car that was parked down the road, out of view.

Don headed home with his tensions gone. His stomach was full, and he'd played some erotic games with a stranger. He might just see her again. *I could always drop by The Simplicity Club and catch up with her, if she doesn't call me first, that is.*

Nine

The Wheelbarrow Ride Home

As Julie lay comatose in the wheelbarrow, Don lifted the handle and felt shocked to find it was a breeze to maneuver the heavy load. He thought to himself, *Cadence! Cadence! One-two, one-two.*

Moving down the sidewalks through the darkness, he got closer with each step, closer to his castle dungeon with his booty and his bride. He considered he could be a modern Attila the Hun, ravishing the countryside. Julie's legs jiggled up and down in unison with Don's jogging.

Shit, just one block to go and wouldn't you know it; here come the headlights of a delivery truck making its morning rounds.

Don ducked quickly into the nearest driveway, all the way into the dark shadows as the truck passed, waiting for his chance to slip back out to the sidewalk to continue his trek. His stamina started to fade as he neared home, pushing the wheelbarrow up onto the lawn and around the corner to the back of the house to stop at the bulkhead.

He had left the doors open, so now all he needed to do was pull the string to put the lights on in the basement. Turning around, he dragged the wheelbarrow toward the ramp.

"Well, here goes nothing." He stepped down, backwards, pulling the wheelbarrow with Julie onto the ramp toward him. But when he reached the fourth step, inertia took over and the weight became unmanageable; he'd overestimated his strength and under-guessed the force of gravity behind her weight. He imagined he could just walk the load down the ramp, but not this time. He found himself at a standstill and unable to step down or push the heavy load back up the ramp. His muscles started to tremble, becoming fatigued and weakened. Finally, he could not endure the weight anymore as he fell backwards.

Everything moved in slow motion as the chariot with his love ran over him. Falling back, his foot got caught in the open riser of the steps, and his head smacked the concrete floor with a bone-breaking "whack." The last thing he remembered seeing was her pudgy feet and legs passing over him. Then he felt phenomenal pressure as the bottom of the wheelbarrow scraped his chest. To make matters even worse, the undercarriage caught his chin, knocking him out cold. It left a three-inch gash as a result of the bolts slicing his skin. The wound peeled back exposing his chinbone. There he hung unconscious by his feet, bleeding like a stuck pig. When he came around, his world was upside down.

Unhooking his foot, he swung down to the floor feeling dazed and dizzy. His head hurt like hell; he sat there pitying himself. Reaching up, he felt a lump the size of a small orange on the back of his head. Although he could stand, he was unsteady and limped over to Julie.

She looked fine, as if there was no problem at all. She was still knocked out with the cloth in place over her mouth. Pulling the cloth aside, what Don saw shocked him. The chloroform had burned her skin, leaving a red rash from her nose to under her chin. He rolled Julie over to the cell, dumping her unceremoniously onto the cot and slipping a padlock onto the cell door latch.

Blood was still running down his shirt as he looked into the mirror. Examining the extent of the damage to his chin, he realized he needed a lot of stitches, but he underestimated how many it would take. He thought up a plausible explanation to tell the doctor as he walked out the door to his truck, because he certainly couldn't tell the truth about what had happened to him.

Ten

To The Hospital

Don was getting dizzy from loss of blood when he walked through the door of the emergency room. He held the skin flap in place with his left hand. The nurse at the reception desk gave a small gasp when she saw this guy with blood all over his shirt, face, and hands. She jumped to her feet, taking him by the elbow and putting him into a wheelchair.

"Hey fellow, let's just take care of your nasty chin problem first. Then we can do the paperwork later. What happened to you?"

"I was standing on an office swivel chair, trying to look for something on a bookshelf when I got off balance," he lied. "I hit the desk on the way down."

The doctor walked in with a smile on his face. "Well, what do we have here?"

He gently moved Don's head back with his right hand, adjusting the light with his left. "Well, we can take care of this, alright, but it will take a few stitches to close." He was being kind, not wanting his patient to get alarmed by how much damage had been done. "Susan, I need a suture kit, Novocain, and a tetanus shot."

He turned, facing the nurse. Susan had a smirk on her face, as she was way ahead of him. She'd already placed the items on the display table next to the gurney.

The doctor covered Don's face with a sterilized cloth that had an opening for the wound to peek through. Taking a large dose of Novocain, he injected a small amount every eighth of an inch. Don felt every pinch as the doctor worked his way through the wound. The doc was humming Beethoven's Fifth as he methodically applied catgut sutures one after another. Don winced every time the doc pulled tight and tied a knot.

"Okay, the inside is looking good. Now let's close the skin. I am going to use very small stitches so that we can reduce the possibility of scarring. It will take more time, but I think you will be satisfied with the results."

Twenty-three small stitches on the outside and fifteen of catgut on the inside made Don's chin look somewhat normal.

"Well, you'll be sore and swollen for a few days. Come back in ten days, and I will remove the stitches then."

Don paid with cash and used a childhood friend's name for the hospital records. Walking to his truck parked in the empty lot, he could see blood on the door and handle. The overhead light went on when he opened the door, and he found congealed blood on the floor and mat. He reached over, grabbing a Herald newspaper, and proceeded to wipe up the blood as best he could, spreading more of the paper over what was left.

His chin was feeling numb from the anesthetic shot, but he knew that soon he would be feeling a lot of pain. *Well, at least I have Julie all to myself.*

He tried to smile, but the stitches pulled every time he attempted to move his cheeks. He tried to smoke, but pursing his lips to hold the cigarette pulled them even worse than smiling. He had to tell himself to drive slowly so as not to attract any attention from the police or anyone else.

He stopped to fill the prescriptions for painkillers and antibiotics at the local drugstore before heading home. While in the parking lot, he thought about the paper trail he was leaving. Even with the fake name, the hospital and the pharmacy people would be able to give a detailed physical description of him, starting with the distinctive chin injury. He had connections to get painkillers on the underground market if he needed them and recalled he had some old antibiotics from his dentist in his medicine cabinet. He figured he'd survive, so he ripped the prescriptions to pieces, dropped them into the sewer in front of the CVS pharmacy, and drove away.

Walking through the backdoor of his house, Don breathed a sigh of relief as he was now home with his new family.

Julie was just coming out of the stupor from the chloroform. She opened her eyes with bewilderment and fear. *Where am I? Why ... why am I here?*

She looked around and saw her makeshift jail cell. It looked as if she were in a basement. The cage was made from thick wood with iron bars slid through holes cut through the center of the boards every eight inches. A heavy iron door was welded together so it locked into itself when closed. She sat on a new mattress with sheets, pillowcase, woolen blanket, and a non-allergenic pillow piled neatly at one end of the bed. She could hear someone walking around above her head. "Hello, Hello? Who is there? Please help me!"

Don walked down the cellar stairs in the dark. When he got to the bottom, he turned on floodlights that lit up the enclosure where Julie sat. It was impossible for her to see anything now the lights were on. They blinded her from seeing who was standing in the dark behind them. Don walked over to the bulkhead and found the ski mask he had ripped off when he came to after the accident. He slipped it over his head and then walked into the light.

Julie sat there with her heart pounding, trying to understand what was going on and how she came to be in this situation. She stared in disbelief at the terrifying figure in the black mask. His chin was covered with gauze as if in an attempt to hide behind an additional mask.

The masked figure extended his arms above his head, spreading them about six feet and holding onto the iron bars. This action made him appear even taller, heavier, and wider than he really was. He just stood there looking at Julie. She cowered, looking down to the floor not knowing what to say.

"There's some fruit, vegetables, and bottled water in the refrigerator when you get hungry. It's over in the corner." His speech was labored from the wounds.

Julie looked around and then touched her face. "My face ... what happened to my face? What did you do to me?" She felt the burn from the chloroform rag.

"Your face? What about my face!" Don said, "You fucked me up real good. I had to get stitches, you cunt!"

Julie was afraid to tell him that she did not know what he was saying about his face.

Sarcastically he said, "Oh, Julie! I am so sorry that happened to you. I didn't realize it would burn you like that! If I had known, I would have knocked you out some other way."

"Knocked me out ... why did you knock me out? Who are you?" She added meekly, "Where am I?"

"We'll talk more about that another time. Right now, I just want to feast my eyes on you. I have fantasized about this for so long!"

Don reached down, feeling his groin. He unzipped and pulled out a half-erect prick that looked somewhat unnatural as it lay there in his large hand. Julie looked down when she noticed what he was doing and recoiled back against the wall. "How would you like to feel this in your juicy, fat cunt?"

Don shook his prick, and it started to engorge larger until it stood at attention and throbbed.

Julie looked on at the display of sexuality in disbelief. Don looked down as he stroked himself. He spoke as if it was not part of him but another individual with its own needs, desires, and feelings.

"Come on Julie, the way you're acting, you'd think you'd never seen a guy's cock before. Have you? Huh? Have you?"

"You're insane ... oh my God ... you're insane! You're nothing but a pervert!"

"Yeah, I guess you could say I am ... am crazy. Crazy about you! I'm beat; I gotta' get some sleep. You can take a shower and freshen up. The tub-shower, sink, and toilet are back there. You can see you have all the comforts of home. After all, this is your home now, that is, until we move upstairs together."

Eleven

The Day After

The next day Don awoke at seven o'clock with his alarm. His chin throbbed a bit, so he popped another of the old painkillers he still had laying around from a wisdom tooth extraction a couple of years ago. The last one certainly gave him a good night's sleep. As he showered, he felt downright giddy. He hadn't been this happy in a long time.

From kindergarten to fourth grade, Don considered himself Julie's protector and came running at her beck and call. If he heard her as much as sniffle or start to cry, he rushed over to care for her.

In the second grade, Julie fell at home on the stairs, cutting her right knee, and it had to be stitched closed. Don felt real pain in his heart when he looked at the wound. It hurt him she'd been injured, and it hurt him even more that he hadn't been there to catch her when she fell. Julie's knee didn't seem to hurt her as much as Don's empathy for her hurt him in his heart and mind. He didn't understand why she made a face at him when he tried to tell her that.

When he first arrived at boarding school, he harbored his anxieties for her wellbeing in his breaking little heart, until he grew bitter and angry after his mother's quick remarriage.

Now things will be the way they were supposed to turn out, Don thought. W*hen we were kids, I knew Julie and I would fall in love and always be together when we grew up. Now I can straighten out what got all fucked up by my dad dying. I'll take care of her and protect her and help her, just as I promised her I would when we were in kindergarten. And she will love me for it ... forever.*

He slipped into his white bathrobe and blue slippers and proceeded down to the kitchen to prepare breakfast. *I think I'll slice some potatoes to fry.*

With that thought, he went back upstairs to fetch the hunting knife from the pants he had worn the night he'd made the snatch. He used it for everything because it had belonged to his father, and it helped Don still feel connected to him, like George was still there helping him. Picking up the empty sheath, Don stared blankly at the stairway for a moment, trying to remember where he had left the knife.

"Oh fuck!" In his mind's eye, he saw himself putting the knife down on the counter at Julie's house before knocking her out.

With a moment's sad reflection, he shrugged off the loss of the memento, and went back downstairs to cook for both of them, just as if they were husband and wife. Then he put on the leather hood he had picked up the week before at the adult sex store in Cambridge. It covered his head down to his upper lip and all of the way back to the lower part of his neck. His stitched-up chin was still in full view. He had removed the bandage and spread antibacterial cream on the wound.

He walked down the squeaky stairs to the basement where Julie was fast asleep, still in an upright position. "Rise and shine – this is the first day of the rest of our lives together."

Julie jumped at the noise; wide eyed she looked at the figure walking toward her with a tray in his hands. At first, she did not see the mask, until he got closer.

"Good morning, Julie. Did you sleep well?" Without waiting for a reply, he continued, "I have some free-range chicken eggs and wheat toast, as well as a fresh sliced orange for you."

"Who are you? Why am I here? Why are you doing this to me? Why?"

"All in good time, my dear. Did you shower and clean up?"

Defiantly, she replied, "Shower? No, no ... what are you talking about?"

"Look Julie, let's make this as easy as possible. Here are some simple rules to follow. Do as I tell you! Every day you clean yourself; then get dressed in the beautiful clothes I chose for you. Keep your room clean and neat. And that yelling for help you did yesterday, you don't NEVER do THAT again, and I'll know, because I'm putting on a noise-activated recorder upstairs for when I leave, so I'll know. You get it, Julie? I said, 'do you get it?'"

Softly, she replied, "Yes – I get it."

"Okay, I guess it's good we got that out of the way. Now we understand where we stand, don't we? You are mine now, and that's the way it's going to be! Now, have some breakfast, and I will give you some privacy. I'll be back in half an hour."

Don went back up to his bedroom. He fluffed up his pillows and got comfortable in his bed. Grabbing his remote control, he turned on the television and settled down. The screen flickered a few times and then the picture came in as sharp as if she was standing next to him.

Julie was gulping down the breakfast as she looked around, expecting her warden to come back any moment. Don watched her; she finished eating and then went over to the clothes rack, picking out one of the two dresses he had chosen for her. She chose the plain dress with cobalt blue coloring he thought would set off her blue eyes, making them even more alluring. She took off her stained, stinking pajamas.

Don watched her undress and prepare for her shower. He could not help but to have already achieved a full, hard erection. He looked down at his penis that was now throbbing. It held itself high above his bathrobe. His heart pumped the blood faster as he became more excited. He also felt the throbbing from the chin injury; this pain only added to the excitement, heightening his pleasure as he watched her shower.

Julie washed her body with the lavender soap and shampooed her hair with the Golden Hue brand shampoo. While they were the finest and most fragrant soaps she had ever experienced, she was too traumatized to notice. She would have enjoyed them if she'd been relaxing in the bath in her own home.

Don had a lot of practice at being able to hold off from coming. He would just let go of his staff when it started to pulsate. After a few spasms, a white drop would seep out of his penis, and he would use it to lubricate himself. After an hour ogling Julie over the hidden camera and halting several orgasms, he rode it through all the way. Stroking hard, he shot with buildup pressure, hitting himself in the face. One glob accidentally landed in his open mouth, much to his surprise. The flavor was nothing that he expected. It had a strange, strong flavor that filled his senses, being musky, exhilarating, and pleasant.

Twelve

Missing Person

In a monotone, the desk officer said into the phone, "Hello, Griffin Police. This is Officer O'Malley. This call is being recorded. May I help you, please?"

"Hi. This is Barbara Leighton from the public library. I need to report a missing person!"

"Hi Barbara, this is Joe."

"Joe, I have a problem. You know Julie who works with me at the reception desk at the library?"

"Sure, Barbara, I know her. She's the pretty little girl who works for you."

"Well, she may not be little, but she is pretty."

"Well, anyway, what's up?"

"Joe, she has not been to work for three days, and I am worried. She did not call in sick, and she doesn't answer her phone. I drove by to check on her. I'm standing on her front porch now. Her car is in the driveway, but she doesn't answer the door. Is there a chance you could send someone to her house to see if she is okay?"

"Sure Barbara, no problem at all. What's her address?"

"69 Mohawk Street."

"Barb, I'll head over there right now."

"Joe, I'll wait for you here. Do you want my cell number?"

"Nah, I got it from the caller ID."

Joe radioed in to the front desk, letting them know he had arrived. He swung out of the cruiser, sticking the keys into his gun belt and allowing them to hang down. Joe walked up to the front door to meet Barbara, who anxiously awaited him.

Joe took his eighteen-inch Maglite flashlight out of the loop where it hung from the left side of his gun belt. He gave the door three sharp raps and waited for some response. Barbara reached over and turned the door handle.

"It's locked, let's try the backdoor."

He gave her a disagreeable glance, and then said sarcastically, "Good idea."

Joe watched for signs that would tell him something was wrong. He looked for jimmy marks on the front door that would have been made by a crowbar, screwdriver, or any other signs of something out of place. Nothing gave him alarm. All of the windows were closed and everything looked normal, until they walked up to the backdoor. "Joe, the door is wide open," Barbara voiced.

Joe stepped inside, drawing his new Glock thirteen-shot automatic from his right-side holster and flipping off the safety. With a loud, controlling voice, he bellowed, "Hello, hello this is the Griffin Police! Is anyone home? Hello!"

Barbara was right behind Joe, bumping into him when he stopped. Joe whispered, "Barbara, wait outside 'til I call you."

Barbara stopped and stayed by the backdoor as Joe moved forward. The hairs on the back of Joe's neck and arms stood up as the adrenaline rushed through every vein and artery of his body. He scanned for the slightest movement in any area of the room in which he stood.

He checked each closet, expecting at any moment an attacker would lunge at him. He was prepared to blow away anyone who would prove to be of danger to him. Joe had made a vow when he was just a rookie that the most important thing was to be able to drive home at the end of a shift.

After checking the whole house as well as the basement, he called out to Barbara. “Well, there seems to be nothing out of place, other than the backdoor being left wide open.”

“But where is Julie? This is not like her at all!”

“I don’t know, but I will put out a missing person’s report and see what we can turn up.”

Joe stood in the kitchen, looking for something – anything – that just did not fit. He checked the locking mechanism of the kitchen door and found nothing out of the ordinary. There was no forced entry.

Then he noticed three white stains on the floor that looked different, somehow unnatural. Joe leaned back against the kitchen counter, just looking around. Then he spied a rather large hunting knife on the counter next to the toaster. It had a mother-of-pearl handle with a nine-inch double-sided blade. Halfway up one side was three inches of extremely sharp, serrated, jagged teeth meant to cause even more damage than the blade itself.

Joe turned to Barbara, “Does Julie hunt?”

“Are you kidding? Julie loves all animals; she wouldn’t hurt a flea. Why do you ask?”

“That hunting knife there on the counter.” He pointed with his chin as well as a nod of his head. At the same time, he bit his lower lip, thinking deeply.

"Barbara, I think we may have a crime scene here. Please step outside so as not to contaminate the area."

Julie's house looked lived in, but it was not the kind of dump some people call a home. It was neat and somewhat in order, other than the unmade bed with a pillow that had no pillowcase. She had photos of family and friends on the dresser and the mantel of the fireplace.

On the counter laid a shriveled-up piece of steak with two large bites taken out of it. Next to it sat an empty glass bottle of Hood milk.

O'Malley used Julie's kitchen phone to call the police station. "Give me the detective's office. Yeah, this is Joe. I'm over at 69 Mohawk Street. We have a missing person problem. Send the forensics department to check out the domicile for prints and other evidence."

Thirteen

Julie and the New Day

Don awoke in the early afternoon after tying one on the previous night. Swinging his legs into the air with momentum, he bounded onto the floor with a twist.

He always slept in the buff. He turned to face the full-length mirror in the corner. He had purchased it at a flea market in Quincy. Admiring his body, he turned this way and that. His hair was disheveled, and he was in dire need of a shave because of the chin injury. "Well, this gives me a chance to see how I'll look in a goatee."

Turning sideways and seeing his beer belly, he immediately sucked in his stomach, trying to look more fit. He thought to himself, *Not bad for a guy in his early thirties*.

Next, he flexed, watching his biceps pop as he took the pose of Atlas. Reaching down, he cupped his sack and ran his hand up to feel his limp but ample member. Walking into the bathroom, he proceeded to brush his teeth and grabbed a quick shower. Now he felt ready to greet Julie and the new day.

She had been awake for a long time, lying there in bed trying to imagine how she could escape. Listening, she heard the water flow through the sewer pipe next to her bed. Half an hour later, she suddenly became aware of the stairway squeaking as Don quietly slipped down to the basement.

In a very cheery voice he said, "Good morning, Julie. It's a beautiful, sunny day outside, but I guess you can't tell that being down here. I got a good healthy protein breakfast for you. I hope you like eggs and bacon. But then again, everyone likes eggs and bacon."

Julie looked up to see a bizarre vision of bare feet, bathrobe, and a hooded head carrying a tray you might see in any lunchroom.

Smelling the food made her salivate as she anticipated having something to eat; she was very hungry and very angry about the meager apples and celery sticks she found as the only snacks Don had stocked into her fridge. She wasn't that big a fan of vegetables – she preferred cookies and chips. Don slid the tray through an opening between the floor and the bottom of the iron door.

Julie grabbed the tray without thought of her situation. Placing it on her knees, she ate. Don watched as she picked up her fork and held it so formally she looked as if she were in a fine dining restaurant. She savored each bit until there was nothing left. She then slid the tray back under the door as if to say, *Please Sir, may I have some more?*

"Julie, don't say anything, just listen to me. I'm gonna' tell you what the ground rules are. This is your new home for the time being, until we get to know each other again.

"Number 1: You must keep your home clean.

"Number 2: Make your bed after you get up.

"Number 3: Hygiene is most important to us. You will shower morning and night.

"Number 4: I have bought the finest beauty products for you to use. You will find them in your bathroom area.

"Number 5: I have purchased you gifts of beautiful clothing you must wear.

"Well, now that you understand what is expected of you, go take your shower now," he ordered in a strong corporal's voice.

Julie looked through the bars at the obvious damage to his face. *Did I do that to him? It's strange; I sense the mask is to cover his identity rather than something he's wearing as a fetish item. There's a caring tone to his voice.*

Don reached down, picked up the tray, and went back upstairs to the kitchen. He could hear the water running downstairs. Going up to his bedroom, he turned on the video screen and sat at his desk, watching Julie. He became intensely aroused with every move she made. After filling the tub, she stripped down and stepped into the hot, soothing water. He enjoyed the movements of her body. Her jiggling and swaying breast got him excited. He turned his head sideways as if it would help him have a better look at the crack of her ass as she stepped into the water.

Leaning back, she closed her eyes and drifted off to another time and place, where she was safe again. Unconsciously, Don put his right elbow on the armrest and leaned his chin into the palm of his hand.

"Son of a bitch, that fuckin' hurts!"

The searing pain lit up his senses with the added pressure of his head pushing on the swollen tissues. It wasn't twenty minutes later when he did it again. He became distracted enough to have forgotten the first mishap. Disgusted with himself and the pain, he turned the camera off and went down to the kitchen to get himself some pain pills and a Bud. After a while, all became quiet. He drank three more Buds as he paced in the living room, anxiously waiting to go back downstairs. An hour later, he returned to the cell door. Standing there, he just looked past the bars. Julie had followed her instructions. Wearing her new white bathrobe, she was looking around at her enclosure and did not even notice that he was there studying her.

"Julie, step over here, and turn around with your back to the bars."

Julie jumped in fear at the sound of his voice. "Who are you?"

"I am your Master! Do as I say; there will be no questions at this time. Do you understand?"

She paused for a moment. "Yes, Sir," she whispered.

"Now do as I say! Turn your back to the bars and put your hands through the bars."

Julie turned around, extending her hands as commanded.

Blood surged excitedly through both of them. For Don, it was because he was taking control of this woman. He felt overwhelming excitement in his mind that shot all through his body into every muscle, but especially into the muscles in his groin. Don gently held each hand as he closed the cold steel loops of one set of handcuffs around her first wrist with a "click, click, click," and then closed the other set around her second wrist, tethering her to a cell bar. He only wanted to prevent her from resisting him.

For her, this exercise was terrifying. Her heart pounded as she felt trepidation, not knowing what might happen next. She thought the slow clicking of the handcuffs was intended to further his intimidation of her, and it was working!

Reaching through the bars, he touched her golden, freshly shampooed hair, burying his nose into the soft sheen as he inhaled deeply. She instinctively flexed her shoulders upward, shrinking her head away, as if she were a turtle trying to escape into her shell.

Unlocking the door, he stepped in front of Julie, standing there with his erect penis protruding past his robe. She froze with utter terror. When Julie felt his hard, hot, pulsating prick slide up against her abdomen, her stomach muscles contracted, and instinctively she shrank away as far as she could. She closed her eyes as if to escape. She kept thinking, *This is all a nightmare ... this is only a nightmare ... I will wake up in my own bed.*

Julie turned away as the masked intruder untied her robe, sliding it back gently over each shoulder. She tried pulling away, but the handcuffs and bars prevented her escape. Don stepped closer to Julie's warm, fragrant body as he took her into his arms. He let his throbbing member slide against Julie's soft lower abdomen, pumping slowly but firmly. He grabbed Julie's hair and pulled her head back, kissing her neck, and sucking just below her left ear. He bit her, lightly sucking at the same time.

The tip of his prick kept sliding into and out of its foreskin, heightening the sensations. She felt this hard, erect part of Don throb and spray his semen upwards so hard it sprayed past her breasts. He did not pull away but continued to rub his body fluids into her skin by rubbing his belly against hers. Reaching down, he stroked himself. Taking what was left in his canal, he applied it to her breasts before suckling them.

Julie tried to resist, but her inner emotions as well as her body sensations took over as she became somewhat aroused. Her nipples started to extend. The large, pink areolas around her nipples turned almost black as they stood out engorged.

When Don saw this happening, he turned, held her head with both hands, and kissed her passionately on her mouth.

Suddenly, he stopped. Pulling her robe closed over her breasts, he exited the cell, locking the gate. He was extremely satisfied with having used her body to give him the euphoric pleasure he craved. She was his orgasm toy.

Julie did not move; she was totally perplexed as to what had just happened. She didn't understand her own reaction; she felt ashamed. She felt shame at forgetting that this was against her will. She was not supposed to want to have his hot prick entering her body, stroking and making her come. But that was exactly what she was craving – her body needed and wanted the violation in the worst way so she could have the release that she needed.

This confused her to the point of total and utter shame. A good Catholic girl is not allowed to enjoy sex outside of the marriage vows, whether she wants it or not. She recognized this was rape and abduction, but on some level she was enjoying it against her will.

Don unlocked the cuffs. Julie moved away from the bars, rubbing her wrists as she walked. He turned and hung them on a nail next to the stairs as he walked up. He just did what he wanted, and he took what he wanted. She was his to please him, and she would learn that quickly.

He reached up and removed the leather hood, placing it on the kitchen counter. Then he took a cold shower to calm down his sex drive as well as wash off any scent that might have lingered on his body.

Dressed in a checkered shirt, blue jeans, and cowboy boots, he bounded down the stairs to the basement door. He called out, "Julie ... hey Julie, I'm going shopping. Do you want anything special?"

Julie whispered to herself, "Yeah, bring me a big knife so I can cut your balls off, you pervert."

Don could not hear what she whispered and hollered out, "Okay, have it your way. If I can't hear ya', then ya' didn't say anything. Food's in the icebox. See you later!"

Fourteen

Crime Scene

Detective Jeff Miller showed up at 69 Mohawk Street with his bag of goodies. He first donned a pair of latex examination gloves. Then he proceeded to take prints off of the backdoor. They were fresh and full of oil – real nice prints showing all of the ridges and swirls. Only problem, they belonged to Julie and not the intruder.

"Jeff, take a look at this knife. It's a Puma – sells for about four hundred bucks! I wonder why he left it behind?"

"He must have forgotten it when he was leaving." Detective Miller gently applied graphite powder to the handle and blade using a very soft, pliable horsehair brush. Removing the excess powder revealed nothing; there were no prints. He put the knife into a large freezer bag so as not to contaminate it. Taking out his digital Sony camera, he took photos of all the evidence.

Joe commented, "It looks as if he was wearing rubber gloves, or he wiped off everything as he left."

"From what I can see, I would say he had gloves," Detective Miller replied.Jeff observed the plate with the dried-out steak and the bite marks in the meat. "Hey Joe, look at that! I'm going to get some fantastic DNA from this as well as a perfect dental bite print."

Jeff also dusted the milk bottle but came up with nothing. Then he took photos of the meat before dusting the plate as well.

"Jeff, why do you keep saying 'he'? Don't you think it could have been a she?"

"Well, from what you were telling me, Julie's a big girl. Most probably, she could take care of herself against another woman. But a guy, he would be able to overpower her. Are there any photos of her we could attach to a missing person's poster?"

Joe turned to his right and picked up an eight by ten glossy photo of Julie. "Here's one you can use."

Jeff took the photo out of the frame and looked at it. "Hey, I know her – she's the girl who works down at the library. A real nice kid ... I hope she shows up okay. It's a shame something's happened to her."

Jeff spent the rest of the day trying to find some other trace of evidence without any luck, that is, until he was packing up to leave. He noticed three white spots on the kitchen floor. He cocked his head, squinted his eyes, and slowly lowered himself into a crouch. Jeff looked at the splash pattern and studied it. Nodding his head, he tightened his lips and bellowed, "Now I got you, you son of a bitch!"

Grabbing his camera, Jeff took photos of the white spots. Then he took three moist swabs from his black bag of tricks and picked up the invaluable DNA. The intruder's sperm had missed Julie's body as she lay on the floor unconscious.

Jeff spoke to himself, "Now everything's falling into place. These guys always screw up! They think they're so smart, but they always leave something behind at the scene of a crime."

The three samples of sperm on the swabs went into three separate plastic bags. He then made notes on each bag, stating where the evidence had been found. Jeff stepped out of the backdoor onto the porch and placed yellow tape across the doorway stating POLICE CRIME SCENE in bold, black letters.

Jeff stood there, looking around at the neighbors' homes. He mumbled to himself, *Someone must have seen or heard something with these homes being so close together*.

Then Jeff spied the candy wrapper in the grass next to Julie's car. The lawn had been cut the previous week, and the paper wrapper stood out like a sore thumb. Once again, the camera captured images for evidence. Jeff bagged it so it could be tested when he got back to the laboratory. He noticed the car locks were still in the locked position but decided as good police work to check for prints anyway. All were smudged beyond recognition.

Since many cases are solved when the police make cold calls to the homes in the immediate area, Detective Miller next went to the house that faced the backyard. Cutting through the bushes, he walked up to the backdoor and pressed the doorbell. After a minute, an elderly gentleman came to the door and peered through the glass.

"Hello, what can I do for yea'?"

Being dressed in plain clothes, Jeff held up his gold-plated detective badge, "I am Detective Miller from the Griffin Police. I would like to talk to you."

The old man opened the door slowly, "I don't know what ya' want, but, I didn't do it!" he said as he chuckled.

Detective Jeff Miller just shook his head and gave the grimmest expression. “I am investigating a missing person’s report.”

“I don’t know nobody that’s missin’.”

“It appears Ms. Julie Booker, the lady who lives over there, is missing.” Jeff turned and pointed to the house behind him, “She’s not been seen for three days.”

The old man’s eyes widened, “No kiddin’! Where is she?”

Exasperated, Detective Miller continued, “That’s what I’m trying to find out! Have you noticed anything out of the ordinary?”

“Like what?”

“Well, different things ... like strangers milling around, yelling, loud noises, dogs barking, anything that is not the same ... you know, out of the ordinary.”

“Nah ... nope,” the old man said, shaking his head. “Theah’s nothing that I can think of right now.” Then he paused for a second, looked up, and rolled his eyes, “Well, come to think of it, the other night theah’ was a racket out back when some dogs got into the trash barrels. The next mornin’ I came out to clean up the mess aftah’ them, but funny thing, the yard was as clean as a whistle.”

“What time was that?”

“I dunno’. Maybe two or three in the mornin’ – it was in the middle of the night! Wait; no ... it was quarter to four. I remembah’ now, I looked at the clock.”

“And which night was it?”

“I dunno’, it was a coupla’ nights ago.”

“Look mister, ah ... what’s your name?”

"Simon Robert Brown and I've lived heah' for all my married life. Me and the missus, we raised five kids. They all went to college. Good kids, yep, good kids."

"May I call you Simon?"

"Sure, sure ... you can call me Simon, that's my name. Just don't call me late to suppah'!" the old man chuckled again.

"Simon, this is very important. Please think more deeply about that night and exactly what happened."

"Well, I'm a light sleeper eveah' since they worked on my prostate. Ya' know that's a very scary thing to happen to ya'. Ya' know, I didn't even know what was going on."

Detective Miller leaned in since Simon was now getting to the details about the night.

"One mornin' I tried to get it on with the missus and nuthin' happened."

Detective Miller cut him off, "Simon, Simon please, let's keep it with the girl next door who we're trying to locate. Tell me about the noise. What happened after that and what did you see?"

"I didn't see nuthin' aftah' the noise. It was very quiet, so then I just went back to bed. But you know, I just couldn't go back to sleep. So I got up and warmed me up some milk. Ya' know, it helps me sleep a little bit better. They say theah's somethin' in the milk that just puts ya' in la-la land."

"Could I ask your wife some questions now?"

"Nah, you can't."

Miller paused, momentarily suspicious as to why Simon wouldn't let him speak to his wife. He asked, "Why don't you want me to talk to your wife?"

"It ain't that I don't want ya' to ... she ain't home. Ya' see, she goes out shoppin' with her sister and them ladies from church, and they all wind up . . ."

Jeff cut him short again, "Oh, I see. Well, here's my card. Could you have her call me the moment she gets home?"

"Sure, anythin' to help out."

"Well, thank you, Simon, you've been a great help. I may come back and talk to you later? Is that okay with you?"

"Sure ... sure, I'll do anythin' to help the law. I ain't like most people. I'm law abidin' ... so is the missus! Ya' know what I miss most?"

"No Simon, what do you miss most?"

"I miss Sergeant Joe Friday on Dragnet. He was the best! Do ya' think he'll come back?"

Miller didn't know what else to say, so he just waved as he walked away. "I hope so, Simon, I hope so."

That evening, Harold Penske led the Channel 7 Eyewitness Report with Julie's photo over the caption, "Local Woman Missing." The Griffin Police notified the FBI, and they added Julie's file to their computer bank, as well as distributed it to all police departments nationwide.

Julie's supervisor, Barbara, made copies of the poster and placed them around town on light poles. She offered a reward of one thousand dollars from her own savings for any information about Julie Booker.

Fifteen

Meeting Up With JoJo

Don wheeled into the Burger Delight parking lot and stayed put for an hour, chain-smoking while he watched the scene. He turned a new waitress away when she tried to take his order and told her he preferred to wait for JoJo. When she rolled by with a tray full of burgers, he hollered out, "Hey, JoJo, come here for a moment."

"Don! What are y'all still doin' here?

She rolled over with a smile on her face that turned to shock, "Oh my God ... Donny, what happened to your face?"

"Uh, I fell down. It's okay, really."

She looked directly at the bandage with empathy, wrinkling her brow. "Oh I'm so sorry you're hurt. Can I kiss it and make it better?" she said in a sweet, loving tone."

Don gave a slight smile and said, "That would work."

"What brings you back so soon?"

"You bring me back. I can't get enough. You know what it's like to have a taste. You want more, and then you want more again."

JoJo said softly and sweetly, "Oh yeah, and what do you want, Sugah?"

"Well, I'll have another order of ... ummm ... French fries, a burger, a Coke, and a taste of you!"

"Donny! I told ya' that my boyfriend would get ma-a-a-d if he heard you say something like that!"

Don just gave her a seductive look as he put his thumb sideways into his mouth, exposing his pearly whites. This movement also called attention to his chin.

JoJo said softly and seductively, "Well, let me get you some food. I'll be right back, Honey."

She came back in about ten minutes with the food, and looking as if she had on a new face. The lipstick was fresh and sharp, outlining her lips. She also wore a hint of perfume that gave Don a rise. She was interested, and she knew that he knew; it was mutual. "Hi Lover, here's y'all food, and it's on me. I get off at one in the morning. Are you going to wait or do you wanna' come back?"

Don sucked both his upper and lower lips into his mouth and bit down on them gently. "I'll wait, Sweetie, I'm not going anywhere!"

Time passed quickly, and JoJo came skipping across the parking lot at one minute past one in the morning. Jumping into the cab of the pickup, she slid across the leather bench seat and touched Don's leg with hers. "Ooooh, I really like that cowboy shirt on you, Sugah. It makes you look even sexier."

He laid down rubber when he pulled out of the parking lot and headed for the Mystic Lakes on the Medford side.

"Donny, can ah touch ya'?"

"Sure honey, I'm all yours!"

Anyone driving behind Don would have thought he was all alone. He slowed down to five miles below the speed limit. After all, there was no rush to get to the lakes to watch the submarine races when he was already getting what he wanted. Taking his merry old time to get to the lake, this was to be one of the most pleasurable late night drives he could remember.

Don dropped JoJo off at her house just as the sun was about to start a new day. She directed the way home, pointing out landmarks so he would not have a problem making it back in the future. As they passed a light pole, neither one of them noticed the poster with the photo of a plump woman on it.

"That one there," she pointed out, "the white cape with the black shutters."

Don pulled to the curb in front of the next-door neighbor's house and turned off the engine.

"Donny, did you have a good time?"

"Oh Baby, are you kiddin'? I'm still stiff and sore!" He sucked in air, creating a reverse whistle as the air passed over his puckered lips. "I want more of you as soon as I can get it."

JoJo replied, "I really don't have a boyfriend. And there's more where that came from!"

JoJo leaned over; Don's zipper was still undone. She went down on him again; it only took him a moment to be at full staff. He did not come again, but she showed him pleasure for a few minutes before retiring to a good day's sleep before her next night shift at Burger Delight. Don drove away after she waved, blew a kiss, and closed the door.

"Oooh!" he groaned as he cupped his balls and smiled. "Now that's what I call a real woman. She knows how to please a man." Running his right hand over his stitched chin, he noticed the aroma of JoJo still lingering on his fingers. He inhaled deeply, passing her essence over his olfactory senses and stimulating him once again. Don stuck his finger into his mouth, tasting her. He shook his head and said loudly, "Man, I got to get me more of that."

Don reached home in thirty minutes and crashed into bed. When he finally started to stir, it was well past noon. He smelled his hand again and got a hankering for a special JoJo burger. He showered, shaved, and dressed in blue jeans with a white shirt rolled up to his elbows. Pulling into the packed parking lot, he circled several times before jumping into an empty spot. Don didn't order over the intercom; instead, he waited for JoJo to skate past and gave his best wolf whistle. He hollered out, "Hey JoJo, over here!"

JoJo turned with a big smile, stopped short, and almost dropped a $15 order.

"I'll be right with you, Sir ... to take your order," she called out to him with a breathless excitement. Skating past Don, she rolled over to a mint 1957 Ford Pickup with a black body and pin striping. She hooked the tray onto the door, made change, and two minutes later, she was at Don's window.

She lunged into the cab and kissed him squarely on the lips.

"Where have you been, Lover? My toes are still tingling." She said this with a flushed smile that covered her whole face. Her eyes twinkled and shined; it was obvious they had something going. There was a magnetism here cooking like a fine stew.

Don thought, *JoJo had a taste of honey, and she wants more, lots more, and so do I.*

"Come back tonight when I get off at 10 o'clock. I want you to fuck me! I want you to fuck me hard! Y'all come back, ya' hear!"

Don felt completely blown away. He had been with a lot of women, but this was unbelievable. *JoJo's just innocent and pure in ever thing she says and does. She makes love for the sheer pleasure and excitement of receiving as well as giving love. I bet that I'm the first guy that she ever let touch her the way I did.*

Don was right. She often went to sleep thinking of all the exciting things she would do to a boy if and when she could. She cupped her hand and made believe that she was touching and stroking him, whoever he would be. Spreading her legs, she cherished the thought of someone loving her for herself.

Don turned the key in the ignition; it gave a pause before it kicked over and started to purr like a kitten. He had a smile a mile wide as he pulled out of the Burger Delight with no food at all, but with expectations of a wild and wooly night ahead of him.

Sixteen

The Sun-Damaged Wedding Dress

Driving through Everett Center, he was lighting up a Camel as he passed a sign that read: "Going out of business, Ruth's Wedding Gowns of Everett, 50% off!"

"Hey, man, that's just what Julie and me need."

He pulled to the curb and walked up to the shop window. The store was closed, but Don peeped inside to get a gander at what was for sale. In the front window, he spotted an outlandish, out-of-style, full-length gown with a train that most women would not want to drag down the aisle.

Just then, Don heard a very sensuous voice behind him say, "Hi there, can I help you?"

He turned around as a beautiful woman stepped out of a new Porsche and headed for the front door. She held out her hand, "Hi, I'm Ruth. Come on in ... I've got a great deal for you. You getting married?"

"Maybe!"

"What's your name?"

"Don ... Don Ricci."

Ruth was about forty-five with short black hair. She stood around five foot five with a nice body. She was the type of woman who, when she moved, every guy within range would turn to look at and think the same thing. Don watched her ass wiggle as she approached the locked door. He thought to himself, *I bet she would throw a good fuck ... and be a lot of fun to be with!*

Ruth unlocked the shop door, turning on the lights as she walked in. "What can I do for you, young man?"

"I'm getting married, and I want to surprise my girl with a wedding dress!"

Ruth's mouth opened, and her face went from a smile to a confused expression. "I've been in the business for twenty-three years, but I've never had a guy buy the wedding dress for his future bride. But ... I guess there is always a first time for everything."

"Well, it's a surprise, ya' know?"

"Well okay, what's her size?"

"I ahh ... I don't know. I guess ... I guess she will be just about ... ummm ... that size! Like that dummy over there with the dress on." Don pointed to the gown in the front window.

It was off white in color and had sun damage on the front. The style was the "big hair type" most women would never choose for their wedding day. It had too many brocade designs, pearl beads, gaudy sequins, and material. It looked like a wedding dress from a 1930s Spanish conquistador movie. It was too much for a woman to be lugging while dancing the night away.

Ruth's right eyebrow arched an inch, "Honey ... I am going to give you such a deal that I wouldn't even give to my own family! My cost for that gown was $5,187.42

I am going to give it away to you for ... for just ... oh, how about $1,000? Cash!"

Don's face dropped, "Gee, I didn't think a wedding dress would cost that much."

Ruth dropped her elegant façade, "Look kid ... I've gotta' empty this store and be outta' here next week. How much are ya' willin' to pay? How much cash you got on ya'?"

Don reached into his back pocket, pulling out the balance of the two grand he picked up at the school. He turned his back to Ruth, pulling out three one-hundred dollar bills, and then turned to face her.

"Look Ruth, I would really like to help ya' out ... but all I have is three hundred bucks to spend. So ... what do you say? We got a deal ... or what?" The two foxes maneuvered, each trying to size up and outfox the other.

Ruth postured as if thinking, then said, "Okay ... okay ... but don't tell anyone about this. This is just between you and me."

"You got it, Ruth ... just between you and me, no one else. That goes both ways."

Ruth quickly stripped the dummy before Don could change his mind. She stuffed the tacky gown into a giant box that could be used to store the monstrosity in an attic for the next fifty years.

"Ruth, please do me a favor and wrap it, um ... in plain brown paper. I gotta' put it in the back of the truck because I gotta' give someone a ride home, uh ... from work."

"Donny, it is my pleasure!"

As Don walked to his truck, he turned around, smiled, and waved. "Maybe we'll see each other again ... some time ... some day!"

Coyly and falsely, she replied, "That would be nice!"

Don lit up a cigarette and tossed the oversized box in the bed of the pickup truck. He needed to pick JoJo up from work. As he started to pull out, he noticed a poster tacked to a light pole. Julie stared back at him with the words "$1,000 REWARD" over her head.

Huh – that's Julie's photo. That's funny!" He sucked hard, inhaling the smoke deeply into his lungs, and then flicked his butt at her face. The super-hot coal hit Julie between her eyes and shattered, sending sparks in every direction. It looked like a mini Fourth of July celebration for Don.

Seventeen

JoJo's Second Time Around

It was ten o'clock on the button when Don pulled into the Burger Delight. JoJo was waiting at the entrance driveway. She had a pocketbook over one shoulder plus a large bag in her arms. "Hi Babe, what you got?"

She smiled, "It's dinner for two at the submarine races." With that, she jumped into the passenger side and slid over to the middle. While climbing into the cab, she noticed a large brown box in the bed of the truck.

"Donny, what's in the box? Is it for me?"

"Oh, it's nothing ... just something I picked up for a friend of mine because he doesn't have a truck to bring it home in."

"Oh."

They had a romantic ride along the winding Mystic River to the Lower Mystic Lake. They listened to music until a newscast came on the radio that led with a story about a missing librarian. Don quickly flipped the channel, explaining, "I hate the news, don't you?"

They passed several parking spots until they found one that was extremely secluded. They hid in the lush undergrowth by pulling past the bushes and out of sight.

"What do you want to eat ... first, Donny?"

Smiling a knowing smile, he replied, "What 'cha got, Baby?"

Teasing him with her pretty smile, she said, "Well I got burgers. I got fries. I got Cokes and ... I got meee!"

"I haven't eaten since last night, and you know the shortest way to a man's heart is through his stomach. Give me the burger, fries, and drink first and save the other ... for dessert."

Don ate with the manners of a truck driver on the run. The fries were between his legs, and JoJo held the Coke for him.

"Donny, what do you do anyway?" she asked sweetly.

Don said, "What do you mean, what do I do? I enjoy life ... I do just what I wanna' do, when I wanna' do it."

"No, I mean ... what do you do, like, for a livin'."

"Nuthin' ... I don't do nothing for a living."

"But Donny, everyone's gotta' do somethin'. How do you pay your bills, buy food ... gas, and everything? What are you ... like in the Mafia or something?"

"No, I'm not in the Mafia or something! My family is what you would call ... kinda' rich. My father was killed in a car crash because the State didn't plow the highway in a major storm. He left behind a sizable estate. So I live the good life. I don't need to work or anything like that."

"Man, are you lucky! Oh ... I ... I ... didn't mean that. I mean ... about your father. I only mean I wish I didn't have to work."

"Well, it's not all it's cracked up to be." Don reached down with his left hand for the electric switch on the bench seat control panel. He moved the seat all the way back, and then tilted it into a prone position, all the while anticipating some good loving from JoJo.

"Come here Baby and give me some sweetness. Give me some sugah!"

When she climbed on top, he found out she didn't have any underwear on. JoJo straddled Don, putting a leg on each side of him as if she were about to go horseback riding. She kissed him softly on his lips. Her hands went to his face, taking care to avoid his chin, and she held him as if he were the most important possession she owned. She then reached down and undid her bra.

Unsnapping the hook between her breasts, she let the bra fall to the sides. Her tits stood firm and high. JoJo's nipples elongated to form delectable treats for him. This sent signals all through JoJo's young and nimble body. Don licked her right nipple first. After a while, he sucked as much of it into his mouth as he could.

She became even more extended as she moaned and groaned with spasms of delight. Don imagined he could taste the enchanting flavor of fluids flowing from her right breast; he then switched to the left one that was begging for him to suckle.

JoJo used Don as her toy. She unbuckled his belt and undid his zipper, sliding his jeans to the floor. His erection gave JoJo a hard place to rub her clitoris and extremely wet lips. She did not put him into her body, but rode against him from the tip to the bottom of his shaft, wetting his scrotum and the bench seat. Don's testicles pulled tight into his groin in preparation for a climax that never came. This went on for two hours.

After many orgasms, large and small, JoJo was at the point of total exhaustion. It was the drug of choice for JoJo and Don. Their brains were super saturated with sexual desire and gratification. When the fire was extinguished, she was totally spent but Don did not ejaculate and was not completely satisfied.

"Oh, my nuts are killing me! My gut feels like someone punched me on both side. You've been having your way with me. I've sucked on your tits forever, and now my balls have 'lover's nuts.' They're fuckin' killing me!"

"Oh Sugah, I'm sorry!"

"You should have fucked me to come off, but it is too late now. I gotta' rest; it's been up for almost two hours!"

"Oh Donny, I'm sorry, Honey! Let me fix that for you." JoJo knelt on the floor between Don's legs. She sucked him into her mouth. Her sweet, wet lips nibbled on his knob as she gently lowered herself down all the way, sending unbelievable sensations throughout his body. She could also taste herself, and that was an additional turn on as she manipulated him.

Don did not move but instead let JoJo do all of the loving. She fondled Don until he started to leak sperm. The sensational flavor gave JoJo multiple orgasms. She sucked him until Don had an explosive ejaculation that lifted his hips off the seat several inches.

Just when he had caught his breath, the truck lit up as if the two of them were in a stage play. Behind the bright spotlight was the familiar red flashing from a police cruiser.

"Oh shit!" they said in unison.

Don quickly pulled up his pants without adjusting his sports briefs. JoJo ducked down to the floor, trying to get dressed as discreetly as possible.

The cop's bullhorn blared out, "NO PARKIN' OVER HERE, GET MOVIN'!"

Don started the motor and backed up slowly, making sure to avoid hitting the police car to his right. Cruising away well below the speed limit, he drove out of sight. When they were sure the cop was not following them, they both looked at each other and burst out laughing.

Later that night when he took her home, at the door JoJo turned and said with a mischievous smile, "Maybe next time you shouldn't be so hungry first. It will be your turn to eat last," she laughed.

Eighteen

Surprise!

It was past two in the morning when Don finally got home and walked down the basement stairs. He had been drinking from the flask he kept in his glove box. He was not drunk but just feeling a little tipsy. He stopped at the last step and said aloud, "Shit, I almost forgot the hood!"

He returned a moment later with his disguise and turned on the floodlights, illuminating the cage. With much exuberance he called out, "Julie, Julie, wake up, Julie ... look what I have for you!"

Julie wore a nightgown from Fredrick's of Hollywood, per order of the Master. She squinted, shading her eyes until she became accustom to the lighting. The masked menace stood there with the large, brown-paper-wrapped box. Julie arose as commanded, coming to the bars.

"I have a gift for you, my Darling!"

With that, he opened the gate, handing the box to her. She had conflicted feelings, and it showed on her face. She did not know what was in the box and dreaded opening it, fearing it could be something terrifying. Her expression divulged what she was thinking.

She asked in a fearful tone, "What's this?"

A woman always wants to receive a surprise – if it is a gift – but not in this kind of surrounding or situation. Julie unwrapped the box slowly. Removing the paper revealed the logo on the box: Ruth's' Wedding Gowns of Everett. Julie looked up at Don for a moment, puzzled. She opened the box and startled when she realized what Don had given her.

"Oh, Master ... I ... Oh ... Ah, it's beautiful ... yes ... it's so beautiful!"

Don took this as approval, as a sign of her acceptance of him. "Julie, I'm so glad you love the dress as much as I do. It cost over $5,000, but you are worth all of that ... and more!"

"But Master, why are you giving this to me?"

"Julie ... we're gonna' get married!"

Julie's face was expressionless as she looked up at his mask. Julie was no fool. Her survival instincts kicked into gear, and she decided to go along with the charade. She knew this was the only way she would survive until she could kill her tormenter or escape his grasp. She held the dress in her lap.

"But Master, the dress is too small. I can't even fit into it."

"Julie, you will in time. I can wait. You will be my dream girl! The girls in Playboy and all of those slut magazines won't be able to hold a match to you."

"Oh, um ... thank you."

"Now, here's a hanger. Put it on the clothes hook over there." He pointed to the end of the cell at an old-fashioned hook on the wall.

Julie walked over and arranged the wedding dress as if she cared about it. Don walked in behind Julie. She heard him, but feigned she did not as he approached her. He stepped up to her, wrapping his arms around her and under her heavy breasts. "Julie, do you really like it ... I mean ... do you really, really like it?"

"Master, it fills me with desire for you when you are so kind to me!" Julie turned around and unbuttoned Don's shirt. Then she opened the bathrobe she had slipped on over her silky nightgown, rubbing her breasts against Don's chest.

"Oh Master, I want you so bad ... you turn me on ... and my body wants you right now," she murmured coyly into his ear.

Don unbuckled his belt; his pants fell to the floor.

"But Master, I am a good Catholic girl, and I must wait until my wedding night to consummate our relationship," she sighed.

Don stood erect through his sports briefs. His foreskin drew taut around his penis, stretching so tightly that the skin appeared shiny. Sensitive to the touch, every time his heart pumped his prick would tremor in unison.

"But let me satisfy you, Master." Julie said.

Don nodded, whispering, "Okay."

She reached down, sliding her hand around his penis and stroking him ... very slowly. She was surprised he was so thick at the base of his shaft. Julie looked down to watch her movements as she pushed toward his balls. The head popped out of his foreskin to expose a large, red knob with a fine ridge, making it look like a prize-winning strawberry.

Don was so excited and taken away with her act of submission that he tensed every muscle in his body. When Julie tightened the skin on the tip of Don's penis, she would inevitably tap against his testicles, pushing them into his body. Julie stroked Don with her right hand and then cupped the throbbing strawberry in her left, twisting it with each stroke. Don started to pant slowly, then faster and faster, until he said in a loud voice, "Oh, Julie ... oh fuck, I've never been stroked so fuckin' good in all of my life!"

Don's prick engorged even larger and harder than before, as a large quantity of semen gushed from the head of his prick. It all seemed to be in slow motion for Julie. She watched as the white, warm fluid catapulted toward her face. Her reflexes were quick enough to pull back as the sperm landed on her neck, while the second, third, fourth and fifth spurts landed on her breasts. Julie played the part well enough to win an Academy Award.

"Master, have I served you well? Did I satisfy you?"

"You bet your fuckin' ass you did. I really needed that. I had such pressure built up in my balls tonight that I really needed to cum. I gotta' get some rest now ... I'm beat. Oh, by the way, thanks ... that was fuckin' great!"

Yeah, you bet it was. You just keep coming on in here without handcuffing me. I'll give you some more, and then when you trust me, I'll give you the last surprise of your life.

Nineteen

Guilty Plans

Don secured the basement, locking the door. He went to the fridge and got an ice-cold glass of milk. It felt so good going down, and he emptied it by the time he got to his bedroom. Turning on the light, he kicked off his shoes, unbuckled his belt, and then let his pants cascade to the floor. Closing his eyes, he crawled into bed.

Even though he was exhausted by his eventful day, he had a problem falling asleep. Down deep, in many ways, he knew he was heading for a disaster. He'd let Julie handle him without cuffs. While exciting, and giving him a rush, somehow it also troubled him.

And then there was the poster and the newscast. While he'd broken the law numerous times, he'd never done anything worthy of making the news before. This both thrilled him and made him nervous. Don's emotions and thinking were vacillating more rapidly than ever before.

He thought to himself, *Maybe I shoulda' tried to date Julie instead of snatching her. Well, if things don't work out ... I suppose I could always just kill her.*

He continued his train of thought, *I could spike her food ... and while she is knocked out, I would just slice the artery in her neck and bleed her out. Then I could cut her up ... put her in a barrel and drop her off the dock in South Boston. It's gotta' be fifty feet deep with all of the ocean liners that used to dock at the pier in the old days. Hmmm ... I'll need to cut six-inch holes all around the drum so the crabs can get in and destroy the body of evidence, ha, ha. Ahhh, that's better. Now I can get some sleep.*

Don slept, but all he dreamt were nightmares. Guilt can be the worst of enemies.

Twenty

Detective Division

Jeff Miller walked up the back stairway to the second floor detective division offices. Joe O'Malley was already there, sitting in a chair with his feet up.

"Hey Joe ... how ya' doing? I see that you're making yourself right at home ... at my desk!"

"I haven't heard a word from you about that missing girl, uh ... Julie Booker. You know, don't let you being a ... ah ... a big dick go to your head. You can still share information with the rest of us peons. What have you found out?"

In an irritated voice, Miller replied, "Nothing, really. I got some DNA samples ... off of the floor in the kitchen and from the steak. I got some nice bite marks with detail imprints from the steak, too. The knife was clean as if he had just wiped it down. I also sent the DNA results to the FBI, but they came up with no hits. The only thing they could tell me is that he is a white male."

"That only means he's never been arrested or applied for a government job or a gun permit. Jeff, did you check with the neighbors?"

Jeff's facial expression dropped, his eyes narrowed, and he looked right through Joe. "Hey, Officer O'Malley, fuck off! And get your nose out of something that does not concern you. You're a patrolman – not a detective. Don't bother yourself with what I am doing or how I am doing it. It was me who went to Quantico and the FBI ... not you! When I got something to tell you, I will. Until then, I won't. You got it?"

Joe let his feet slide off the desk; his boots hit the floor with a hard thud. He stood up, grabbing his gun belt with both hands and lifting to adjust it back onto his hips.

"Any time you want to step out back of the station and have a go at it," Joe bristled, "you just let me know – so that I can kick the shit out of you and teach you some manners!"

"Joe, it'll never happen. I'm your superior, and someday I'll be your chief. You hear that? By the way, I am treating your statement as a threat and insubordination. I won't stand for that, you hear?"

All went quiet. Joe didn't say anything; he just stood there and thought to himself, *I better get out of here before I deck that son of a bitch and lose my job! I got to get back on the street.*

Joe turned without a word and trotted down the stairs quickly. His boots danced and echoed until he opened the basement door to the parking lot.

Twenty One

Prize Fishing

Julie waited until all was quiet, and then she started to look over every inch of her prison. She spoke in a whisper – it helped her think if she envisioned she was talking to someone else.

"Okay, now let's see what we can find for a weapon. I don't see anything in here, do you?"

"Nope, I don't. But what do you call a weapon – a gun, a knife, a club or what?"

Julie answered herself back, "Well, anything that can cause some damage quickly, cut him badly, or something to break the lock on the cage door, keep looking," she commanded, "look everywhere – check the bars, the floor, everywhere!"

Getting up, she slowly walked around searching for an opportunity. "There is always a point of weakness, always."

Grabbing the bars, she shook every one independently. They were all rock solid. Each bar went from the floor to the ceiling. On the floor, there was a two-by-four plank drilled with holes to receive the bar. The same thing was on the ceiling. Across the middle, halfway up, a crossbar was welded, making everything extremely sturdy. He had not installed anything new on the other walls. They were just the old brick and cement foundation. The bath and toilet sat in the corner of the basement with no privacy walls to separate them from the rest of the cell. The only window was across the cellar on the other side of the basement. Looking outside the cell, Julie noticed something shiny on the floor about fifteen feet away, outside of the cell area against the wall at the bottom of the stairway.

"What is that?" she whispered.

She stared at the object for quite a while until her eyes finally made out the details of what she was looking at. "It's a hook! It's a hook of some kind with a handle. Yes, yes ... if I can get that, I could straighten it out and use it as a spear."

Again, replying to herself, she said, "But you need a rope." Julie looked around and saw the heavy string she had slid off the wedding dress box lying on the floor. "Yes, that will do just fine."

Remembering an old Zorro movie where the hero made his escape by taking the rope that supported the mattress and tying a throwing weight to it in order to hook the cell keys, Julie untied the knots and worked all of the kinks out of the string. Then she looked around for anything she could attach as a weight.

She was in luck. Just outside the bars on the floor, Don had forgotten the remainder of a box of six-inch spikes he had used to build the cell. She smiled to herself, "Hey Julie, those will work great. Now find something that you can use to bend the nail into a hook."

Sitting on the bed, she noticed a space between the bar support and the rafter as she looked up.

"I bet you could bend these nails just by slipping them into that crack," she chatted to encourage herself. She jumped up and slid the nail into the crack. Taking the string, she looped it many times until it was as strong as any rope. Then she wrapped it around the nail and hung all of her considerable weight from it until the spike bent.

"There you go ... now it has an L shape. Move the nail further in, hang on it once more, and you'll have a hook shape." Grabbing two more nails, she repeated the process.

"Okay, tie all three together now and you'll have a treble hook." Julie tied the string around her left wrist so she would not accidently lose grip of her improvised self-rescue tool. Then she put both her hands outside the bars, holding the looped string in her left. With her right, she threw the make-shift hook. It sailed through the air, landing with a clunk not far from the metal tool she sought.

"Okay, that's the way. Now do it again." Retrieving the contraption, she cast it again. So many times, it hit so close, but the hook would just slide off again and again.

"Hey, doesn't this remind you of that game with the glass box stuffed full of dolls," she said, "with the three-fingered claw that almost never captured the toy." She paused a moment, since the point of the conversation with herself was to help her think through this situation constructively, and now she had dampened her spirits with this last comment. Deliberately recasting into a positive thought, she said, "But this will work for you!"

This exercise went on for hours, until she could not throw anymore. Fatigue had set in and her arm muscles felt sore. "Okay Julie, time for a break."

She said this to keep herself from giving up after this first, fruitless session.

She wrapped the string and hooks up neatly, hiding them under her mattress. Staring at the ceiling from her bed, she continued the conversation with herself.

"Hey, who the hell is this guy anyway? Why did he pick me? Where does he even know me from?"

"He must know you from work ... at the library. He seems to be treating you as if you were his cave woman – he saw you, wanted you, and took you!"

"Aside from kidnapping me, holding me against my will, and using me for a little sex, he hasn't hurt me, and he seems to kind of care about me," she replied.

All of a sudden, a loud voice shot out of Julie's mouth. "What the hell are you talking about? What ... are you an idiot? That son of a bitch has taken away your life! You'll never be the same. You're a marked woman for the rest of your life, and another thing – who the hell will ever want you now? No self-respecting man would ever want a woman who has been tainted the way you have been tainted. It's entirely your fault for flaunting yourself."

She fought back. "Flaunting myself? I didn't do anything! I was asleep in my own bed, and he stole me!"

The voice shot back, "Yeah, yeah, then try explaining this ... why have you given into all of his ... whims? You're kind of getting off on this kinky S&M shit. You never knew you were a perverted slut before, did you?" The realization of this possibility about herself really stung.

"Whims, what whims have I given into? I'm manipulating him until I can get him where I want him. Then I'm going to kill him! Wait and see what I do to him!"

Julie lay back once again, gazing at the hook across the basement floor. She closed her eyes and envisioned her movements. She was like a prizefighter in the ring. She could see each movement. Her shoulders flinched ever so slightly as she destroyed her tormentor in her mind.

Twenty Two

Trimming Down to Fighting Weight

Something was happening to Julie, something she had wanted since she was a young woman. She was losing weight, although not of her own accord. All of the food her captor was bringing to her was from the discount food store; every meal was a diet frozen-food dinner, and her only snacks were vegetables and fruit.

She longed desperately for the same familiar comfort foods she had grown heavy on. It wasn't like being able to eat whatever she wanted, whenever she wanted it, and she normally relieved her stress by eating. Although she had plenty of good reasons to kill the Master, some days she fantasized about eating a gallon of chocolate chip cookie dough ice cream with a whole package of Oreos crumbled over it as she sat on his stiff, dead body. At those times, she knew she was being petty, and the food should have been the least of her worries, but she understood what people meant when they said they'd kill for a cookie.

Days were turning into weeks; she even lost track of the current month. Her daily practice of hook throwing gave her some calorie-burning exercise.

One day Don walked down to the basement carrying a rather large rocking chair. He said, "I'll be right back."

He returned with an assortment of books from a large discount bookstore. "Look what I got for you. Since you work in a library and you always loved reading, I knew you would enjoy these."

He had picked out what he thought she would be interested in reading. However, he chose the books by the cover rather than by the content or author.

Julie sat on the bed whenever he approached to make him feel more comfortable by appearing submissive. The face behind the mask smiled as he eased himself down into the rocking chair.

"I think it's time we get to know each other once again, aside from the little frolicking and having a good time we've been doing. You know, we used to be good friends many years ago."

Julie looked at him and squinted, trying to understand what he meant.

"Don't do that ... it'll give you crow's feet. Didn't anyone ever tell you squinting will give you crow's feet?"

"Yeah, I heard that somewhere. What do you care?"

"Julie, I don't want you to age before your time. After all, you're mine now, and I want you looking good for a long time to come. So now, tell me all about you."

Astonished at his inquiry, she stammered, "I ... I don't know ... what you want ... or where to start."

"Start from the beginning. Start from kindergarten."

Julie thought, *Kindergarten? What's so special about kindergarten?*

As Julie started to describe her experiences in grade school, she never mentioned anyone by the name of Donny, Donald, or Don. He tried to remain calm and not let her see his growing annoyance. Maybe she was saving the best for last, waiting to tell all about her best friend, the love of her life.

Relaxing her guard a little as she reminisced, "Now, in the fourth grade, I had my first boyfriend."

Don rocked back and forth rhythmically with his elbows resting on each armrest. His thumbs were under his chin as if to support his head, with his index fingers placed together to resemble a church steeple which rested on his lips. He hung on every word coming out of her mouth.

"His name was Hunter Roberts. He sat behind me at the school assembly," she commented. "He was such a sweet little boy."

Don twitched under the mask at the mention of the other boy's name, yet he couldn't remember the boy. At first, rather than anger, he felt sorrow mixed with pain and heartbreak he did not understand.

His mask was now more frightening to him than to Julie. She feared him less and less as she became aware she was gaining psychological control of the situation. Once Julie had progressed to high school with no mention of Don in her recollections, he stopped her in midsentence. He snarled, "That's enough for now!"

"You said we used to be good friends many years ago. What did you mean by that? Why do you want to know about my childhood? Did we know each other?" She leaned forward as she peered at him, "Do I know you?"

"Keep that thought ... you keep that thought, and just maybe someone will come to mind!" Anger welled up within Don as a defense against the emotional hurt he felt. "You know, you're making me irritated because you're not remembering correctly."

Don stood up and unbuttoned his shirt, placing it on the back of the rocker. Then he kicked off his boots and slid down his pants. All he wore was the mask. "Assume the position!"

Her eyes widened with fear and confusion as she shirked back. "What ... what do you want me to do?"

"Kneel on the edge of the bed and put your head down on the pillow against the wall."

She did as she was told. Don opened the cage door and approached Julie from behind, flipping up her dress and sliding his penis under her and then rising to meet her lips that were already starting to engorge, becoming wet with anticipation.

Getting raped is not my idea of a good time, but why is my body getting aroused? She felt guilty and confused by the jumble of terror and excitement. Her heart picked up the pace and beat faster. She breathed more quickly as all of this was happening all at once.

Being so wet, he encountered no resistance at all as he placed the tip of his prick into her. He did not dive in like so many inexperienced juveniles but continued to stroke and tease her with just the enlarged tip. The movements were short, one-inch thrusts that gave Julie immense pleasure as her folds rolled over the ridges of Don's penis.

Somehow, she forgot for the moment she was being raped. At this point, all she wanted was to feel the fulfillment of an ecstatic orgasm. Julie wanted more and pleaded with a whisper, "Deeper, deeper ... hit my hot, sweet spot ... fuuuccckkk me ... fuuuccckkk ... me!"

She started to push back harder and faster so they both were in unison. She climaxed hard, forcing vaginal juices past her lips, soaking Don's balls until it dribbled down his legs.

Don had yet to come, so he grabbed her by the hips, continuing to stroke her with full jabs of his penis. Each time Don's balls make contact with her ass, they made sloshing and clapping sounds. Stroke after stroke he continued, until Julie was on the verge of another orgasm.

Her mouth opened; she breathed hard. Her mind envisioned his prick entering her. It was then that Julie opened her eyes and looked back and through her legs. There in full view she watched Don's balls and most of his prick stroking her. She felt in another world, mesmerized – enjoying sex for the sake of sex and the pure animalistic pleasure that was now taking over. All that she wanted was to have this feeling. Her mind and body were in unison searching for ecstasy. She screamed, moaning as she buried her face into the pillow as her mind went wild with the endorphins firing all together.

Don could not hold off anymore. His balls, in full firing position, tightened up into his body. The thrill exploded from his knees through his body to the top of his head. He pulled her hips back, compressing his prick as deeply as possible into her, both physically and mentally. He envisioned his penis stiffened, throbbing repeatedly as he emptied his sperm into Julie as if she were to be the only woman to continue the human race.

Julie rolled onto her right side into a fetal position, totally confused and exhausted. She had just had the best sex from someone who was raping her. He took her his way, with no regard to her feelings or desires. But she had never had such intense, exciting sex with anyone before. It was as if someone had injected heroin into her; she knew she would want more of the fix so she could have the same high over and over again. She felt anger, humiliation, and shame simultaneously with exhilaration and gratification. It was as if this was the taboo that everyone speaks of, the desire to fulfill one's natural instincts as often as possible for the sheer pleasure in and of itself.

Don lay down next to her, engulfing her body with his arms and legs. They lay together for almost an hour, not saying anything while so many thoughts raced through their heads as they rested in a semi-conscious state. Don awoke first; moving his hips, he found himself momentarily stuck to her backside. He reached down, peeling his foreskin away to reveal his quite ample penis. He was not as proud of its size as of his ability to use it to gratify himself and every woman he bedded, or so he believed.

The water pressure in the house dropped as they both took showers. While he felt completely satisfied with his physical conquest, she attempted to wash away the results, in shame, both physical and emotional, of being raped. Julie was angry and wanted revenge. She knew she was his captive – nothing more. In her predicament, she believed the best thing was to ride the rapids until she could reach calmer waters.

She grabbed the showerhead off of the hook and dialed the spray over to a steady, pulsating stream of water. She squatted and directed the stream of warm water past her lips into her violated body, washing away secretions and sperm. It was therapeutic, both physically and mentally. She may have continued the procedure longer than necessary, but the sense of being sanitized eased her mind. She couldn't allow herself to contemplate the possible ramifications of his seed actually being deposited within her. She could only focus on survival.

Julie could not hear any movement from upstairs. *He must have left the building,* she thought. *Sometimes he'll be gone for a day or two and then show up all matter of fact. That masked man is no Lone Ranger.*

Julie was going to make it stop – for good. She reached under the mattress for her fishing hook. With so much practice, she'd gotten better at casting. Each time she threw, the claw landed right on target but invariably slid off the hook. Today would be the day; she could feel it in her bones.

After his shower, Don continued his nap in his own bed. A tapping noise gently awakened him. A puzzled expression crossed his face. "What the fuck is that?"

He wondered what had stirred him when he heard a tapping noise coming from the basement. He reached for the remote to turn on his candid camera that prior to this had provided him with perverted fun. He rustled the covers, and then leaned over to shuffle through the bedside table. "Damn, what did I do with that thing? Shit, I can't turn on the TV without it!"

Julie was in mid-cast when she heard footsteps coming down the stairs from above her. She quickly retrieved the fishing line and stashed it under her mattress. Panicked and not sure why her captor approached, she picked up her fork from yesterday's meal and started tapping the bars at the same tempo as her casting. Don came downstairs shirtless.

"Darling, what are you doing? You woke me up from my nap. I needed some shut eye after you took me like that. By the way, where did you learn to holler, moan, and groan like that? You are such a fuckin' turn on."

"I don't know."

"Come on, no one fucks like that without havin' a lot of practice. Oooweee man, you're like a wild woman! I think I must have woken up some wild bitch in you. Honey ... did you fuck other guys like that?"

"No, Master, I guess you bring it out of me. I've never been turned on by anyone like that before. I have always been kind of a wallflower. I'm kind of embarrassed by the way I acted."

"Embarrassed – you shouldn't be embarrassed."

"I hope I was not too forward with you." As Julie blushed and looked away, she thought to herself, *Hey, not bad ... I bet I could get an Academy Award for this performance!*

"Well, Sweetie, you've never met a man like me before. I'm a man's man. I can fuck you every which way from here to Sunday. I can lay you, relay you, and parlay you. I can make you my toy, playing with you all day and night. How do you like that? Huh ... well, how do you like that?"

"Oh, I like it just fine. You turned me on, and I will always be here to serve you."

Don felt smug and powerful. He had heard exactly what he wanted to hear. "Julie Baby, I gotta' go out and meet someone. Don't wait up for me. I don't know how late I'll be out. See you later."

Don bounced up the stairs. He grabbed a handful of Oreo cookies and some milk for lunch. He started to walk out of the backdoor when he glanced at the mirror on the wall. The sight greeting his eyes scared the shit out of him as he jumped back in alarm – his own reflection in the hooded mask. He pulled it off, laughing all of the way to the pickup truck. He sat in the driver's seat sipping milk from the carton and twisting the Oreo cookies apart, licking the sugar filling just like he had when he was a kid.

Julie waited for the motor to start and listened as it faded into the distance. She dropped her shoulders and exhaled a long sigh. *Damn, that was too close!*

She tried to squelch the images of what might have happened if he had discovered her secret, and she turned her energy back toward her escape. She lifted up the mattress, got her hook, and wrapped the string around her wrist. Tossing the hook, she watched as it flew through the air almost in slow motion. The string followed the hook with the hoops unraveling off her hand in a perfect, even flow. The hook bounced off the wall, landing on the curve of the metal.

Julie puckered her lips and tilted her head. "Not a bad pitch. Okay, come to mama!"

As Julie pulled the string, it became taught from the resistance of the heavy tool. Slowly the handle turned and started to scrape across the floor.

"Come on baby! I need you in the worst way ... come on ... come to mama ... please?" It slid across the floor until it touched the bars of the cell with a soft click.

At last able to breathe, Julie inhaled deeply and reached down to pick up her hard-won prize. This was the first time she could see it clearly. It was an old bailing hook with an oak handle that fit neatly into the palm of her hand. She extended the hook through the bars and, with one quick motion, pulled it back with such force she even surprised herself.

She struck the bars repeatedly with the hook, sinking it into the imaginary figure.

Each time she visualized the hook buried deep into the Master's back, again and again with so much fury and hatred – for kidnapping her, for starving her, for raping her, for teaching her things she never wanted to know about herself. Julie screamed, "An eye for an eye, you dirty bastard, take that ... and that!"

Tears welled up in her eyes, not tears of fright or sorrow but tears of anger and revenge. Each time the hook crashed into the bars with a deafening ring, the stream of tears gushed down across her face, spattering the floor at her feet. The Master started to take form. The sinister mask fell to the floor as the hook pierced his skin, going into the soft cartilage of the neck and spinal cord, crippling him. Julie envisioned the imaginary corpse falling to the floor in a crumpled state of pain and then death. She turned away, letting the hook swing on the bars as she let go of it.

Falling onto the bed, she sobbed uncontrollably, feeling so alone and desperate. Depression descended upon her, and she fell into a deep, hypnotic, much-needed sleep.

Twenty Three

Hunger

Don drove to the Louie's Italian Pizza Shop at Revere Beach. Even though it was out of the way, it was the best Italian pizza sold by the slice. Owned by some Greeks who came over on the boat in the '50s, they never changed the name or the style. Don parked across the street; he smelled the sumptuous aroma of garlic and oregano in the air. There was almost no traffic as he walked up to the door. Demetrious was the owner, pizza man, dough maker, and cashier. The bell hanging on the knob jingled when Don walked through the door.

"Gimme' two piece-o-pizzas and an ice tea."

"That'll be $5.50. Here kid, 'dese just came outta' da' oven."

He reached over, grabbed the slices, and slid them onto a paper plate by the crust. Don's mouth started to water as he watched the drops of butterfat glisten as they rolled off the pizza and soaked into the plate.

"You wanna' larger drink for only a quarta' mo'?"

"Yeah, sure ... why not?"

"Here ya' go, kid."

"Hey Demetrious, why do you work so hard? You could slow down ... you don't need to work so hard, being here all the time. You got so much cash stashed away downstairs you don't need to do this."

"Cash ... what cash? You kids is all alike. You tink dat' money grows on trees. Well, it don't! You gotta' bust your ass for it. You gotta' keep wha'cha make and add to it. Da' money ... da' money ... you gotta' make da' money!"

"Yeah ... but you never go on vacation."

"Don't need no vacation. I come here from Greece when I was a kid. I didn't have a pot ta' piss in when I got here. My broder' and me had five bucks between us. We worked hard. We didn't get no fucken' vacations. We saved, we scrimped, and we stole from dat' fucken' grease ball what owned 'dis place."

Demetrious laughed from the bottom of his bloated, fat belly, "Me and my broder' ended up buyin' 'dis fucken' place from him ... wit' his own money! Ha, ha, ha!"

"I heard this joint was owned by the mob."

"Ya' it was! He was one of 'dese mob guys connected wit' da' boys from Rhode Island. You woulda' t'ought he woulda' been more on da' ball ... but he had more cash 'den God. He didn't even notice 'dat we was skimmin' him!"

"Weren't you afraid he would catch you?"

"Nah, we knew he wouldn't. We'd buy extra flour on da' side each week and make our own dough. He was never da' wiser."

Don picked up the fresh pizza, folding the crust in half for stability. Then he lifted the warm, high-butterfat cheese, and delectable sauce into his mouth, biting down into the fresh, crispy dough. The delicious mozzarella was just a bit salty as it slid down his throat. He took bite after bite until the first slice was gone, and then he took a long chug of his extra-large ice tea. Don turned back to the pizza man and said, "Demetrious, you got the best pizza on the Beach ... no ... no, in all Boston! What's your secret?"

"You know what they say? Well ... if I tell you, I gotta' cut your tongue out so 'dat you can't tell uh'ders!" Then he laughed the same sinister laugh as before.

Don just gave a half smile, "No thanks, just the same."

He picked up his second slice, grabbed his tea, and walked out the door.

"Hey ... I'll catch you later." Then Don mumbled to himself, "That fuckin' Greek bastard, I bet he would try if he could."

He crossed the street and sat on the seawall, enjoying the early summer weather as he watched the seagulls sailing on the hot air currents coming onto the beach. He watched as they moved their wings ever so slightly, hovering in the same spot in the air. His stomach felt full and satisfied. With the leftover crust in his hand, he tore off bits and threw them into the air at the gulls in flight. One particular gull must have been an old timer. He had perfected the art of gliding. Even though there were a dozen birds on wing, he bullied the others. Only he fed from Don's generosity.

Twenty Four

Checking Out Robin

Don had built up a thirst from the pizza despite the extra-large ice tea. He wanted to feel a cold Bud Beer washing his throat clear of the film now coating it from the greasy pizza. This was just as good a time as any to catch up to Robin at The Simplicity Club. After five minutes of twists and turns down streets that were originally old cow paths, he hopped onto Route 1 headed north. There overlooking the highway was the Hilltop Steakhouse with a crowd wrapped around the corner of the building. Don thought, *I wish I hadn't eaten the pizza now that I smell the beef coming out of their kitchen vents.*

One more mile, and he pulled into the overflowing parking lot of The Simplicity Club. The crowd was filing past the two huge bouncers. They checked IDs just to make sure everyone was legal. The crowd was a mish-mash of blue-collar workers, truckers, businessmen, lawyers, doctors, and drug dealers. Then there were the girls who worked the crowd. There were always plenty of guys who got their horns up and would pay for a quick hand job from Mary Palm and her five sisters.

Don cut the line, walking right up to one of the bouncers. The guy stood almost seven feet tall and must have tipped the scale at close to four hundred pounds and nine inches taller that Don.

"Hey, is Robin working tonight?" Don looked up at him, showing the bouncer no hint of intimidation. He gave the man a look as if he could see through him all the way to the back of his fat skull. The big guy looked down at Don as if he were a munchkin from "The Wizard of Oz."

"Yeah, she's dancin'," he grunted.

"I'm a friend of hers," Don extended his hand, reaching up to shake hands. Between his palm and thumb, he held a folded up twenty-dollar bill. The big man extended his huge mitt and engulfed Don's hand so gently it shocked him. It was as soft as a piece of marinated meat. A smirk raised the right side of the man's mouth as he felt the bill being palmed. He didn't say anything else but just nodded his shaved head to the left, giving Don permission to cut the line and gain entrance.

Don stepped into the blackness of the club as loud music blared from surround-sound speakers. The smells of cigar and cigarette smoke intermingled with that of stale beer – the unmistakable aroma of a club. The only lights lit the stage, which was surrounded by men young and old seated in bar chairs. They watched the show fantasizing what they would do, if only they could do what the beckoning women were suggesting.

The actual reality was but a few steps away, behind a curtain and through the green door that led to the back room. The hookers who worked the patrons were not the dancers but a separate group of girls who were on call. They were younger than the dancers were. The back room was where they started to work their way up the ladder.

It was good cash for a few minutes work. The prices varied for services rendered. After watching the dancers for an hour or so, it only took a moment for any gentleman to shoot his load. The girls would bet on who could make a patron come the fastest. They would perfect the twist and turn with a slow stroke, then work the head when they felt it pulsating. They made three hundred bucks or more a night.

Don took a seat at the stage when a man left for the back room. Not a minute had passed when he heard a sensuous voice whisper, "What can I give you? Oh ... I mean what can I get for you, Honey?"

Don turned to his right, sticking his nose straight into a pair of delicious breasts bulging out of a pushup bra.

"I'll have two of those. Are they rentable?"

She smiled, "While that is entirely possible, would you like a beer first?"

"Yeah ... give me a Bud."

"Be right back." When she turned, walking away showed the only thing she had on her backside was a G-string covering her front. Her ass was small and muscular; she looked fantastic in the high heels that accentuated her strut. Don lit up a Salem Light while he waited for his beer. Although not his favorite cigarette, it was a freebie from his teacher's lounge caper, so he couldn't complain too much.

The Master of Ceremonies started his introductions. With his drawn-out words, he sounded like the barker who introduces the fights on television. "Gentleeeemannnn, may I have your attennnnntion. Now I would like to present one of our most popular dancers here at The Simplicity Club, our own heart stoppin' Miss ... R-R-R-O-O-B-BIN!"

Music from "Saturday Night Fever" blasted from all four corners of the room. Robin stepped out, and the crowd went wild with wolf whistles, howls, and applause. She was the headliner and the toast of the town at The Simplicity Club.

Robin smiled and leapt into the air, coming down into a full split. That move turned every guy on as each imagined her coming down on his own erect penis. A roar went up and dollar bills flurried down onto the stage. In no time, she was completely naked but was entirely professional in her presentation as she took hold of the brass pole on the right end of the stage.

She seemed to levitate to the top of the pole with her feet touching the ceiling. Ever so slowly, she rotated round and round the pole until her shoulders almost touched the floor.

Miraculously, her high heels swung under her. She continued to dance and swirl until her finale, where she did the splits once again. Then rolling to her knees, she pivoted herself slowly, showing her anus and vagina to the men who sat at the edge of the stage; she was not more than one foot from their faces. This special treat caused a showering of singles, fives, and ten-dollar bills to flood the stage. She smiled a glorious smile. Kneeling down, she swept all the money into her arms. Taking a final bow to the crowd, she backed off the stage with her booty in hand.

For the whole time Robin danced, Don was mesmerized by her movements. He knew this was show time for Robin, and the performance was all that mattered to an artist expressing herself. After she finished, Don started making his way over to the entrance of the dressing rooms but was blocked by a rather large bouncer.

"Hi ... I'm Bobby," he said, looking down at Don. "Where do ya' think you're going?"

Don had to look up even though he was six foot three. "Backstage – I'm a friend of Robin's, and she asked me to drop by to see her."

"Yeah, you and ten other guys. You wait here! What's your name?"

"Tell her it's Don ... Don from the beach ... from the other night and the clam dinner. She'll remember me."

Bobby just grunted and walked toward the dressing room. The bouncer could not fit through the doorway unless he turned sideways and ducked his head to slide through the opening. He disappeared into the darkness.

Robin was seated, putting on a new face. She was finicky about her stage presence and always wanted to look perfect.

"Hey, Robin."

She glanced into the mirror, looking back to the door where Bobby poked his head into the room. "Yeah, Bobby ... what's up, Baby?"

"There's a guy who wants to see you. Says his name is Don from the beach ... ya' know 'im?"

Her face lit up, "Yeah, tell him I will be out in a while. Bobby, tell him to order me a bottle of Champagne. He's got to pay for the privilege of having a drink with me!"

Robin then looked back into the mirror and continued to touch up any imperfections she could find.

Bobby came out from the dressing room door and walked up to Don. "Hey, Don ... she says she'll be out in a few. Oh, by the way, she says she wants a bottle a' Champagne."

Don gave him a nod and sucked his lower lip. He thought to himself, *A bottle of Champagne? What is she fuckin' thinkin'! If I gotta' buy her a bottle of Champagne, I wanna' take her outta' here. Go someplace that's dark, cozy ... with just the two of us.*

Don leaned against the wall, still nursing his first bottle of Bud. He watched two more shows, chain-smoking the entire time, before Robin came out in her street clothes. She wore a white shirt with the tails tied in the front with a double knot and the same threads of jeans cutoffs she had on at their first meeting. She had braided her black hair, and it hung across each shoulder as if she were a squaw. This outlined her features as if she were in a frame, with her being a painting. Robin sashayed up with the same walk she had the first time he had seen her.

"Hi, Donny, how ya' doin'? Did you see my show? What did you think?" At that point, she wrapped her arms around him and gave him a peck on the cheek.

Don was caught off balance with the barrage of questions he needed to answer before anything else could transpire. "Robin, you're fantastic and so talented – you're the best dancer I've ever seen. How are you able to do those splits and hold your weight upside down on that pole? God, you're the best! Really," he said with a chuckle, "you're the best!"

Robin blushed, "Why Donny, you're so kind and caring. Thank you, thank you! But I work really hard at it. As they say – the only way to Broadway is practice, practice, and more practice."

"Yeah, I know what you mean."

"Donny, I'm so thirsty, could you get me a glass of Champagne, please? Come with me ... we can sit over here." Robin led the way to the table in the corner, far away from the stage and riff raff. "Donny, I'm so happy you've come to see me at work. What took you so long to get here?"

The waitress walked up to the table, "Can I get something for ya' to drink? You want another Bud?"

"No, give us a bottle of Champagne." The waitress cracked a grin as she walked away. Don turned to Robin once again to answer her question, "Well, it really wasn't that long ago. But then ... I guess maybe that means ... you missed me?"

"Sure I did! I'm glad you came."

The waitress returned with the bottle of Champagne and two stemmed glasses. "Well, here goes nuthin'." She pushed the cork with both thumbs; there was a loud report as the cork shot for the ceiling, bounced off the wall, and landed in Don's glass. She hollered out, "Hey, I got a hole-in-one! How 'bout that?"

They all laughed, and it cut the tension. As Bobby shuffled past their table on his way to the front door, he said, "I've worked here for five years, and I ain't never seen nuthin' like that." Don reached over, took the bottle from the barmaid, and dismissed her.

Looking across the table at Robin, Don felt quite the man. Here he was having Champagne with the headliner of The Simplicity Club, even though it tasted like cheap, young booze. He could feel eyes of envy staring at the both of them.

"Donny, I've been thinking about you a lot, and I'm glad you finally came to see me. That dinner we had by the bay ... it was very romantic."

"Robin, I couldn't get you off my mind. I didn't want you to think I was comin' onto you, but I'm glad you opened up to me. Come on – let's get out of here and get somethin' to eat."

The barmaid sensed they were finished and walked over with the bill, "All set folks, ready to go? Here's your tab."

Don looked at the bill, and his eyes popped open. "Hey, Sweetie, you must have mixed up my bill with the whole bar tab. This is $199 for a bottle of ginger ale. What are you, fuckin' nuts?"

Bobby was at his post next to the door, but because Don was yelling, he noticed the misunderstanding. He walked over to smooth the waters before things got out of hand. "Hey Donny, you got a problem? What? You don't want to pay your bill? Did you order Champagne or not?"

Don bristled at this jerk using his childhood nickname – it was one thing for him to tolerate Robin calling him by it affectionately, but another matter entirely for a man to call him by the diminutive name, trying to belittle him. "Yeah ... I did, but not two hundred bucks worth. Not like that was Dom Perignon! What are you trying to do, fuck me over?"

Bobby gave Don a look that could kill – this was business. Don was going to pay ... one way or another. "Look it, Donny, you're a nice guy. I don't wanna' see you get hurt. Just pay the fuckin' bill. Then after, you go get laid with Robin. Don't screw with me ... or I'll have to break you up! I'll break you up bad, because that's my job. You hear me, Donny? I said ... do you hear me?"

Robin hung back toward the table, letting Bobby work his mark. Fuming inside, Don looked around and sized up his situation. He felt angry, but he wasn't crazy and realized this wasn't the time or place. Don dug into his back pocket, pulled out two one-hundred-dollar bills, and handed them over to the barmaid.

"Where's my tip?"

Exhaling through his nose, Don almost snorted. He pulled a twenty from his front pocket and slapped it into her hand.

Bobby said, "Thank you, Donny. I'm glad we could settle this like gentleman. You're welcome to come back anytime and visit our Robin. Now, why don't you kids go have a good time! Go ahead, and forget all of what just happened."

Don stomped out the front door, making a beeline for his pickup truck; he had an uneasy feeling he was being followed. Spinning around, he pulled out a ten-inch switch-blade. Pressing the button, a heavy blade sprung out of the handle and stopped with a click. Any man would have known he was in trouble after hearing that sound, just like a rattlesnake before the strike.

"Donny, it's me, Honey, it's me!" She screamed, as she put both hands up in the air as if to surrender. "It's me, Donny!"

"What the fuck is going on? You rip me off and then you want to take me for more?"

"No! No! Sweetie, that wasn't me – that was not me! That was Bobby! I don't call the shots here – I just dance here – really, Sweetie!"

Robin stepped closer, lightly pushing the blade aside. She kissed Don on the lips, sliding the tip of her tongue into Don's mouth. He responded by placing his right hand with the switchblade behind Robin's back, pulling her closer to him and kissing her passionately. His left went to her ass and slid past the strings to caress her exposed flesh. Robin reached down, groping Don's groin and massaging him.

This was very erotic and arousing for the both of them. Maybe danger and death was just around the corner, which only heightened their newfound relationship. Each wanted more: more sex, more danger, and more excitement. Robin moaned into Don's ear, "Donny ... Donny, more ... more ... Donny give me more!"

Don pressed the button again, and the blade retracted back into its handle with a loud click.

She had just put on a new face before she had come out to see Don. Now that they were in the open air, Don could smell the cheap perfume and taste her lipstick as he held her in his arms. Sliding his hands to her waist, he lifted her onto the hood of the truck. She spread her legs, wrapping them around his waist and locking him in her scissors grip. She was there for the taking, and she let Don know it. So many guys in the club would have loved to have been in Don's position; it would have been a dream come true.

"I gotta' go," he mumbled, his brain overcoming his lust as he realized their exposed and dangerous position. "This ain't neither the time nor place."

"But Donny, I want to be with you right now, not later!"

"Robin, I said I got to go. I got bad vibes with the likes of Bobby and what just happened. I'll catch up with you later."

With that, Robin reluctantly released Don and slid off of the hood onto the gravel parking lot.

"I'll catch up with you later, Robin. Give me your phone number, and I'll call you later, okay?"

"Okay! Got a pen?"

Don reached into the console of the truck for a pen and paper and passed them over to Robin.

She said, "Here's my address and phone number. Don't forget about me. You better call ... I'll be waiting. It'll be worth your while ... I bet you!"

As the engine roared to life, Robin reached through the window. With both hands, she took Don's head, pulling him closer and kissing him on the lips.

He left Robin standing in the parking lot and pulled into the traffic of the highway. "That fuckin' bitch, I'm going to fuck her long and hard. You bet I'll be calling you, you cunt."

Don was beyond irritated at what had just happened at the club. "Bobby, that fucker, he really pissed me off. He stole two hundred bucks from me!"

Don was seething. "He hasn't seen the last of me."

As he headed home by way of Route 1 South, he kept seeing Bobby in his mind giving him the ration of crap.

"I ought to use my aluminum bat on that fat fuck. I can just see him on his knees, begging me not to hit him again. I'll just smack him on the top of his head to teach him who is boss. Fuck it – I'm going to do it. I'll whack, whack, and whack that son of a bitch. He'll be sorry he ever gave me shit."

All the way home he could see Bobby in his mind and just what he was going to do to him when he went hunting for him. "When he's on the ground, I'll break his knee caps just for good measure."

Twenty Five

Bum's Rush

Don was still angry from the humiliation Bobby dealt him the night before, but today the sun warmed Don's body as he walked down Park Street. On the corner, he saw a guy holding a paper bag sign that read:

"I WILL WORK FOR FOOD!"

"GOD WILL ALWAYS BLESS YOU!"

Something clicked in Don's mind. For some reason, he got mad. He watched the bum work the crowd; the more he collected, the more Don wanted to destroy him. Watching the bum for about ten minutes, he became increasingly agitated, entertaining the desire to beat and rob him.

This con artist had a blank expression and a two-day-old beard. His eyes showed he was in need of a fix and had not eaten that day. When the stoplight turned green, the traffic rushed forward, causing the sidewalk to fill up with pedestrians waiting to cross. The bum turned and held the sign over his head.

A gorgeous, young, redheaded office worker dressed in a two-piece gray suit reached into her purse and gave the panhandler a crisp five-dollar bill from the paycheck she had cashed on her lunch break. The mooch's facial expression did not change as he palmed the fin, sliding it into his pants pocket with the other two hundred he had scammed that morning.

Down deep in his gut, Don was getting aggravated as he watched the bum. He felt the same anger as the previous night when he could not take his aggressions out on Bobby. It was as if his drug was violence, and he craved a fix.

Look at that no good, filthy, stinking, lazy scammer mooching off society. I should make him think twice about panhandling again.

Getting an adrenaline rush, he visualized exactly what he was going to do. He felt in the mood to hurt somebody, and this random bum would be the one. His mind flashed back to the improvised punching bag made from an oversized stuffed duffel that he had hung in the basement of his step-dad's mansion, where he took out all his anger after his father's death and his mother's hasty remarriage. Don felt as ready to kill now as he had felt then. He'd seen where the panhandler stashed the money. The bulge made his right pocket larger than the others.

Don cased the area, looking around; no one was paying attention to him. He noticed an alley between Northern Trust Bank and Bob's Sub Shop. Grabbing the guy by the back of the neck, he lifted him as if he were a rag doll. The bum responded with wide-eyed fear and compliance.

Don leaned forward, whispering into his ear, "Boston Police, fucker ... you're under arrest for panhandling!"

Bostonians don't like to stick their noses into other people's affairs and mind their own business; they ignored what was going on. Don pushed his target away from the crowd. The bum protested by saying, "Hey, I ain't done nothin' wrong. I'm just tryin' ta get a couple bucks for somethin' ta eat!"

"Really? Come with me!" He lifted the bum up by his shirt and pushed him toward the alley. The con looked like a dancing puppet with his toes just touching the ground. Don kept pushing and pulling him until he slapped him into the corner at the far end of the alley, far away from any prying eyes and ears.

"You know better! You know that you're breakin' the law! Don't you?"

"Hey, everyone's doin' it! No one cares! Why don't you go pick on someone else?"

"Because I want to pick on you – how much money you got?"

"I ain't got nuttin'! Honest! Things is real bad!"

Don reached down and grabbed his pocket where the bulge of money was stashed. He pulled with such force the pocket ripped right off the pants. Don held the wad under the guy's nose and said, "What the fuck do you call this? You call this nuttin'?"

"Hey, you can't do that! That's against the law!"

"Hey asshole, I am the law!"

"Yeah? Lemme' see your badge – you ain't with no cops!"

"You want to see my badge? I'll show you my badge!"

Don stepped back, planted his right foot firm on the ground, bobbed his shoulder, and fired a punch, nailing the bum right in his solar plexus. The air gushed from his lungs with a sudden whoosh as the guy started to collapse. The bum tried to cover up by bringing his arms together over his face and chest.

Coiling back like a snake, Don smacked him again. He planted his right foot firmly on the ground and threw a punch with such speed and force it pushed the bum's hands away from his face. His left fist met the man's gasping, defenseless jaw. Fear took over, and the panhandler no longer tried to defend himself. The guy saw stars just before his head cracked hard on the bare white bricks behind him.

Blood gushed out of a three-inch gash in the back of his head; he was unconscious before he hit the ground. Don stepped back and admired the blood track on the wall. He tilted his head and thought to himself, *That looks like a modern progressive piece of artwork by Pollack.*

Don glanced down the alleyway to see if anyone witnessed what had happened. People just walked past minding their own business, oblivious to the bum's fate. Putting the money into his jacket pocket, he checked the bum's clothing and found nothing else of value. Turning, he walked nonchalantly to the sidewalk, looking right and then left. He spied a knapsack lying under a postal box. As he passed the box, Don casually bent down and scooped up the goody bag. Again, no one noticed anything.

Suddenly, the heavenly aroma of fried burgers with onions overwhelmed Don's nose. He realized he'd worked up quite the appetite from giving the guy a beating. Following the delicious scent, he walked across the intersection and into the Greek hamburger joint on the next block. The restaurant was quiet but for a few retired men huddled in one corner arguing about the Red Sox, who had blown the pennant once again.

Don walked straight into the men's room. Emptying the contents of the bum's bag into the sink, he found a Buck

Knife, a half-eaten baloney sub, a pot pipe in the form of a Labrador puppy, a bag of grass, discount coupons from the Sunday Globe, and a paper bag with a thick, red elastic band holding it secure. Opening it, he found eight hundred dollars in twenty-dollar bills. He clipped the knife onto his belt. The money he folded in half and added to the cash already in his pocket. He put the large bills on the inside and covered them with one-dollar bills on the outside. Don was street smart; he knew better than to flash a wad.

Dumping everything else into the trash, he washed his hands in the sink. Now being like Pontius Pilate cleansed of his deeds, he ordered two cheeseburgers with a small Coke to go.

Don wolfed down the first burger and took a long suck from his drink. Leaving the trash on the table, he headed out the door and walked down the street, away from the alley, with the Coke in one hand and the second burger in the other.

In the distance came the sound of a siren screeching its way through traffic. In no time, it flew past at an ear-splitting decibel. Don stuck his fingers into his ears to protect them. The woman standing next to him did the same thing. He looked a little silly with a drink and burger on each side of his head. Once the ambulance had passed, they both put their hands down at the same time.

She turned to Don and said, "I wonder what the rush was all about? The way they were moving, you'd think it must be a life-and-death situation. Oh, look, they stopped just down the street at the alley!"

The EMT's took their time getting out of the vehicle. One of them walked into the alley. A few minutes passed, and he returned with the bum holding onto his arm.

The woman said, “Will you look at that? Do you see that guy holding his head?

“Yeah, what about him?”

She said, “He’s running away from the medic. Good God, what is this world coming to? They try to help people and they don’t want help; others, they will try to steal the last nickel you have in your pocket!”

Don just smiled knowingly and nodded his head, “The guy’s probably got a bad heart, do you think?”

He took the last bite of his burger, and then slurped what was left of his drink, dumping the cup on the ground.

The woman said, “Hey Mister, you’re not supposed to throw your trash on the ground.”

Don smiled, turned, and said, “Yeah, I know. Why don’t you pick it up?”

Twenty Six

Hooking the Big Fish

Don walked over to the nail that held the cell keys. He wore his familiar headgear. "Julie Baby, I've been out seeing a lot of other girls, but they don't turn me on the way you do!"

"Where have you been, Master?"

The coffee maker alarm sounded off with a ping. It was on the table next to the keys. Don poured two cups of black java and walked over to the rocking chair next to the bars. He slid Julie's cup through the bars, placing it on her night-stand. "Here is a fresh cup of the finest Arabian coffee. You know ... you can't beat Arabian coffees. They are the best. The Arabs were the first to drink coffee. Have you ever tried drinking it? Or you might say chewing it. Arab coffee is so thick your spoon could almost stand upright and you gotta' put sugar in it, a lot of sugar."

"No, I don't like coffee. Thank you anyway."

"You asked where I was. Why do you want to know?"

"Well, you said that you were somewhere and that you saw other women. I was just trying to make some small talk, that's all."

"Yeah, but they aren't like you. You're special; you haven't been around like them."

"Special? How am I special?"

Don started to get turned on, and he fidgeted in the rocker, biting his lower lip. "Well, like ... well, you haven't given me a blow job yet! How would you like to try that?"

"Why do you ask me sometimes and other times you just take me, doing what you want?"

"Well, it all depends on how I feel. Right now I feel like having you take me by giving me a blow job, sucking me off very slowly."

"Yes Master, I would like that. You must have ESP because I was fantasizing about just that!"

Hearing Julie talk like this excited Don, and his penis started to engorge before he could get it out of his pants. Reaching over, he grabbed the keys and opened the door. Unzipping himself, he exposed his hard, erect member. Julie reached for his penis. Placing the tip into her mouth, she stroked him as she forced herself not to gag from disgust. Don was not the first man that Julie was ever with, but she played her part as the sexually naïve Catholic girl well. She asked him for instructions. Don willingly told her just what to do.

"Master, please, sit on my bed and close your eyes," she purred.

Don obeyed Julie and did exactly what she instructed. She continued the give him pleasure. He dropped his guard, focusing on his own arousal.

Julie reached under the bed and palmed the bailing hook firmly in her right hand. Quickly, she raised the hook up and over Don's left shoulder, aiming the point at the spinal cord in the middle of Don's neck. Don was oblivious to anything that was going on and only concentrated on the sensations that were building up to an orgasm.

Suddenly, Julie pulled with all of her might. The point of the hook catapulted toward Don's neck. She had made her attack, and the movement of her hand made the shank of the hook ride against Don's neck, but it was off the mark. Instead of the spine, the point sank into the soft flesh and muscle on the left side of Don's neck. It was as if a bee had just stung him. The sudden shock to his nervous system made him ejaculate prematurely; then the tremendous pain set in.

Don's eyes sprang open; his jaw dropped but no sound came out. He exhaled a huge gasp as if the wind had been knocked out of his lungs when the sharp point found its place. Julie had expected him to keel over dead, just as the phantom had in her many practice sessions. She pushed the handle, and the point slid out of the puncture with blood gushing onto the wall and bed linens. Once again, she pulled hard; once again, the point missed the spine, sinking into the ligaments, muscle, and sinews of his left upper back. Don sat there looking confused with an expression of disbelief.

Once again, she tried to destroy her foe. This time the point found Don's shoulder blade. It did not embed as deeply this time because it became lodged in the bone. This wound felt as if the bone had been broken ... but it had not. The hook got wedged into the bone, and it held tight. Julie could not continue her unrelenting attack.

Don jumped up with such force he catapulted into the air, striking his masked head against the ceiling rafters. When Don's feet landed on the floor, he swung his right fist with an uppercut motion. This reflex caught Julie on the left side of her jaw, lifting her off of the floor. She sailed through the air, as if in slow motion, landing with a crash against her wedding dress. The dress teetered back and forth until it slipped off the hook and landed on top of her, leaving only her bare feet exposed.

The pain ... the pain was like nothing Don had ever experienced in his lifetime. He screamed, "What have you done to me? So this is it ... this is how I die? Fuckin' Bitch – I'm not ready to die! Not here or now!"

With that, he reached back, trying to remove the hook, but it held fast. With every step he took toward the door, the pain intensified. Staggering through, he reached back with his right hand, pulling and locking the cell door.

Don reached up with his right hand and felt the hole the weapon had made. He then stuck his finger into it to stop the bleeding. He left a trail of blood as he found his way to the kitchen. Don stopped and looked into the mirror, examining the figure standing there. It had its right hand over its left shoulder with blood dripping down to the elbow. He saw what was causing the pain.

There in the mirror was his bailing hook that he had misplaced a few years ago. With his right hand, he tore off the mask and closed his eyes for a second in excruciating pain and disbelief.

This was the last thing he ever expected from Julie. He did not think she was capable of such an attack, as he thought she had started to love him again.

Now he turned his attention to the stuck bailing hook. For a moment, he contemplated the idea of driving to the hospital with it still in his shoulder, but thought better of it. Don placed the handle against the frame of the door, gritted his teeth, and leaned forward to push the imbedded point out of the bone. The handle slipped, and he knocked his head against the wooden door jam. "Son of a bitch!"

Each time he pushed the hook, he screamed in pain, "I gotta' get this outta' my fuckin' back!"

The handle would slip, and he would bang his forehead again. In frustration, he backed up five feet, running with force into the doorframe. This time he met with success. The hook released its hold, sliding out of Don's back and onto the floor with a clatter. Vertigo set in as he lost consciousness from the pain. He thought it strange to see the floor rushing into his face. He felt no pain as he landed hard beside the hook.

When he came to, Don struggled to his feet and clung to the backstairs handrail as he walked slowly and carefully to his pickup. Sliding behind the wheel, the motor turned over as easily as ever, and he popped the clutch, screeching out of the driveway.

He figured it too risky to return to the Winchester Hospital. The distance was about the same to Mount Auburn Hospital in Cambridge, so he banged a left onto Route 2 East. The pain intensified with each imperfection in the road. He tried to avoid shifting so he wouldn't have to use his left hand to drive.

Why am I so nauseated and dizzy? Shit, I'm losin' my fuckin' blood! He felt weak and fought to keep his head up with eyes on the road. *Fuck, why are those streetlights so bright?*

It seemed all his bodily functions were malfunctioning. His head and neck throbbed so bad that he wove as he drove. Finally, he pulled up the driveway to the emergency door.

A black nurse met him as he staggered through the door. This one also bypassed the paperwork and had Don lay down on a gurney. They were accustomed to seeing gunshot wounds nightly at this ER. In the emergency ward, the Dominican intern walked in with a huge smile and, in a thick accent, repeated the line all the emergency room doctors seemed to say to their patients. "Well, well, what do we have here?"

He lost the smile with his first glance at Don's blood-soaked clothes. Taking the flat-tipped scissors, he slid them under Don's shirt and proceeded to cut his clothes away from his body. The blood had started to congeal and crust up. The doctor stopped for a moment when he reached the first hole in Don's back, and then continued to cut the clothing away.

"Nurse, looks like he's been shot." Parting the bloody garments, he continued, " " " There are a total of three bullet holes. There are two in the back and one in the neck. Looks like you been shot up real bad!"

"No, no," Don groaned, "Some guys jumped me and stabbed me with something sharp."

"Nah ... you been shot okay. I seen lots a' bullet wounds and this is a gunshot okay! Just let me probe and see how deep the round went. I'm gonna' give you a shot of Novocain to numb the areas and make you somewhat more comfortable."

Don didn't feel the needle at all, because he was in far more pain than a little needle prick. The doctor took his forceps and probed the hole to find the bullet. He expected to hear a metallic sound but found nothing in any of the wounds.

"I can't find any of the rounds. Let's have some X-rays just to see if there is anything I missed."

"Doc, I told you ... someone stuck me in the fuckin' back," Don sputtered, ". . . with something sharp. I would know ... if I was shot! What do you think that I am ... a god-damn idiot? I would know ... when I was shot and ... when I was stabbed!"

After being X-rayed, Don was rolled back into the examination room. The doctor said sheepishly, "Looks like you've been stabbed with something wide and sharp. There is a lotta' bleedin' and hematoma, but other than that you look fine. I'm gonna' give you a transfusion of a pint a' blood, a tetanus shot, a few stitches to close the punctures, and you will be as good as new in a few days. The scapula thats your shoulder blade bone – was pierced ... but it will mend just fine."

Then the doctor pointed to Don's neck, "You're a very lucky young man, Senor. A few inches to the right, and it woulda have hit your spinal cord. You woulda' been killed, or at least crippled for life."

The doctor called, "Nurse, where are the admittance forms?"

"I just rushed him in because of the emergency. I'll do them now." She picked up a computer tablet, "Now, what is your name and can you give me your insurance information, Sir?"

Don paused for a moment, "I don't have any insurance, and so if it's okay with you, I'll just pay you cash. How much do I owe you?"

"Well, I guess that's okay. Now, what is your name and address?"

"I told you ... I'll pay cash!"

"Yes ... I know ... but I still need your name and address for the police report."

"I don't need a police report. I don't want to make a police report. Now how much do I owe you?"

Overhearing, the doctor interjected, "I am sorry, Senor, but the law is the law we must report all acts of violence. But have it your way if you want. You can talk to the police when they get here. 'They will be here in a few minutes."

Don hedged, "Okay ... sure, sure ... I'll talk it over with them. Hey, where is the bathroom? I gotta' go real bad."

The nurse replied, "Over there ... down the hallway, third door on the left."

Don walked very slowly due to the great deal of pain from his injured shoulder. Each step he took moved the wounds, muscles, and ligaments, causing pain to wrack through his whole body. The holes, though closed, were swollen and throbbed as if each were a beating heart in and of itself.

Just as he reached the bathroom door, he glanced back and saw he was not being observed. Even though he was shirtless and bloody, he kept on walking, slipping out the emergency room door. Once behind the wheel of the pickup, he was out of sight before the police turned up.

Ten minutes later, the state trooper pulled up to the hospital and strutted through the emergency room door as if he was still in the Marine Corp.

"Hi Doc, wha'cha got for me? I hear someone was shot."

"Yes Sergeant, at first I thought he'd been shot. But then I figured out he was stabbed. I patched him up okay. He's in the bathroom."

"What's his name? Who is he?"

"He won't tell us, but said he'll tell you."

"You bet your bottom dollar he will! Where is he?"

The nurse led the way to the bathroom door and pointed. Ever cautious, he slid his Mag-lite off his belt loop and pushed the door open. Flipping the light switch on as he stepped inside, the trooper didn't see anyone. Cautiously, he stepped over to the toilet stalls, pushing each one open in preparation of doing his duty and finding out what had really happened to this sponge.

He mumbled, "I bet it was a drug deal gone bad." After the fifth toilet stall, he stepped back with a stupefied expression on his face, "He ain't here."

Twenty Seven

Tell Me a Lie

Julie cringed with a breathless mixture of hope and dread as she heard someone come into the building and walk down the stairs. Julie thought, *Could that be him?* She closed her eyes praying, because she could hear only one set of footsteps.

She tried to reassure herself, *Maybe it's the police ... they probably just sent one officer around to check the house.*

Then she panicked, *Oh my God, if he's not dead ... then I will be!* She started shaking as horrors ran through her head. It flashed before her eyes, with all of the gore, blood, and guts being discarded. *Oh, God, please let the pain last only a moment. Let him kill me quickly.*

Julie's face turned ashen when she saw the hooded figure make his way down the stairs. He walked down very slowly, clinging to the handrail. Each step was as deliberate as the step before. The pain he felt was nerve racking. He tried to prevent his back and neck muscles from moving with each step. She could see that she had hurt him badly. The pain was in his eyes as if he were looking for some pity from the very person who had almost killed him.

Don carried a gift for Julie, in spite of her savage attack that had almost cost him his life. Even though he wore his hooded mask, his lower face showed the pain and agony. The extensive injuries to his body were minor compared to those to his ego. He now felt he was walking on eggshells around Julie, but that also added to his excitement and challenge.

Don gently eased himself into the rocking chair. "I bought you a gift. I must apologize for my behavior. You must have been very angry ... to have done what you ... did."

Julie stood motionless, and her face did not show any signs of expression. She neither looked away nor did she show fear. Don passed the present through the bars and set it on the side table. She considered what kind of trick or trap might lie within the tinseled box.

"Julie, tell me a lie."

Julie just stared at Don. Her mind spun as she tried to keep cool, but she was still trying to figure out Don's latest play.

"Julie, I said to tell me a lie!" he said in a demanding voice.

She squinted her eyes, wrinkled her face, and tilted her head toward the box. She spoke with anger and resentment in her voice. "Oh, Master, I am so pleased you have brought me a surprise gift."

With that, she did not move but continued to stare Don down with a grotesque look of disgust.

In a softer tone, he said, "Julie, tell me another lie."

Now leaning toward him, she spoke in little more than a whisper. "Master, I love when you treat me the way you do."

"More Julie, more, keep telling me more lies."

Still leaning forward, she tilted her head. "Master, oh Master, I fell for you the very first time you raped me! You made me swoon and lie awake thirsting and waiting for your return."

Snapping back at her, he demanded, "More ... tell me more."

Each lie triggered something in his mind. He wanted and needed more humiliation. He was acting like a dog being beaten, yet going back for more punishment, licking the tormentor's feet again and again.

Posturing her shoulders back and lifting her head as if she were a politician, her eyes were weapons in and of themselves, slicing into his body and destroying the very essence of him.

Sarcastically she stated, "I yearn for the day that I will be your wife and will get to submit to all of your whims any time of day or night!"

He screamed, "More, damn it, tell me more. I didn't say to stop, did I? Tell me more fuckin' lies!"

She continued lying for what seemed to be hours until she was at a loss for words. She stopped and just looked at him without expression. She had beaten him at his own game.

He was depressed and gazing at the floor, thinking thoughts that he did not share with her.

Finally, he got up slowly and quietly and walked up the squeaking stairs, a confused man for the moment.

Twenty Eight

Stake Out

The summer passed before Don felt like his old self again. During that time, he saw to Julie's needs, bringing her food and things like toiletries and books, but he barely spoke to her. He never approached her for any kind of sex.

He felt emotionally crushed by her attack, but he did love her in his own broken way. He couldn't bring himself to harm her, but he couldn't risk setting her free, either. He thought of her kind of as an animal he had captured and removed from the wild, and now he was stuck with the responsibility of caring for his wild pet. He hoped with time perhaps he could mend their relationship, but for now he had to focus on healing his own body. He believed he would win her love later.

Don couldn't turn his immense anger from the attack toward Julie, so he kept thinking of how Bobby had belittled him. Bobby had taken away some of his manhood, and he felt ready to give the man he considered a fat slob some payback. Tonight was the night to start stalking him.

Don grabbed a pair of binoculars and drove to the club, which was located across the street from a large, bankrupt shopping mall. The parking lot gave Don a perfect view of the club. He spent three weeks casing the joint, watching the patterns of the patrons and workers. Hundreds of butts scattered the ground from his chain-smoking during the observations.

Bobby was always the last one to leave the building. The club's parking lot had one spotlight left on 24/7, and he parked his sports car under the light as a deterrent to anyone who wanted to damage it. Bouncers always staffed the front door and watched the lot at all times. Don decided Saturday night of Labor Day weekend seemed as opportune a time as any to take revenge.

He dressed the part of a cat burglar with a black shirt, faded black jeans, and black sneakers topped off with a black knit cap. He went into the garage, retrieving his Little League aluminum baseball bat from the box in the corner. He cradled it lovingly. His dad had bought him the T-ball miniature bit when he first started playing baseball because the wooden bats were too heavy for him to swing. He held it in both his hands as his memories rushed back to the Christmas morning when his father told him, "That's right, Donny, Santa was here last night, and he left you a Louisville Slugger. You'll be the number one hitter in Little League."

Walking to the driveway, he took the familiar stance he had always taken when he was at bat, the stance his father taught him as team coach. He visualized centerfield and swung the bat with vengeance; he could see the hard ball flying with such ease, going over the fence. His instincts took over, and he started to take a step toward first base when he snapped back to reality.

"Well, I guess it's time!" Don started to get physiologically pumped as his adrenaline flowed. Driving toward the club, he visualized what he planned to do to Bobby.

One whack to Bobby's knees would be a cool thing to do. He'll be limping for the rest of his life. While he's on the ground, why not break his arms to put him out of commission for even more time?

Don drove straight to the mall parking lot and cut the engine. The club was jumping with a large, mixed crowd standing in queue, trying to get into the building. The sounds of the club violated the night air and echoed off of the mall walls. Picking up the binoculars, he watched with anticipation.

There were more women than he expected. Then he spotted the new sign advertising Ladies' Night Extravaganzas. This was a mixed couples' night with a live sex act on stage. The women seem even more excited than the guys, perhaps because of what the night's expectations might turn out to be. Couples were going to their cars to take swigs from open bottles, pop pills, and smoke joints before going inside. The drinks and drugs on the outside were cheaper than the ones in the club. The crowd size stayed the same because of cars milling in and out, to and fro; when one left another one drove into the lot.

It was two o'clock in the morning when the bar closed. People filed out of the bar and started their cars, heading for the open road. The only ones left in the club were the cleanup crew hustling to mop the floors, empty the trash, and restock the bar so they could get home. One hour later, everyone had left except for Bobby. It became quiet and eerie as a graveyard with only the one light illuminating Bobby's taffy-apple-red Corvette.

Reaching over, he grabbed the bat with his right hand while he opened the driver's door with his left. He held the bat close to his leg so if someone saw him walking they would not notice he was carrying anything.

Don paused at the guardrail of Route 1 for a moment. He glanced to check for traffic, but the highway looked like a massive, empty parking lot. He switched the bat to his left hand so he could steady himself at the railing with his good right shoulder. Springing into the air, he landed softly on the black pavement. Don smiled with excitement; the intrigue of sneaking around in the middle of the night blended with the anticipation of the revenge he was about to dole out.

Making his way up to the left side of the building, he slunk into the shadows at the rear of the club. The rank smell of decomposing urine permeated the air. The moon was full, so he could see where he was walking with no problem. When he reached the other side of the building, he stepped up to the large oak tree that was at the apron of the parking lot. He squatted on the ground and waited. Mosquitoes buzzed around his head. Some landed on Don's neck, feasting as he ignored them.

Half an hour passed, and then Don heard a noise. Bobby stepped through the side door. Don could hear his smoker's cough as he inhaled deeply from an unfiltered Camel cigarette.

"I gotta' stop smokin' these fuckin' things ... they're killin' me." With that, he inhaled once more before flipping the butt into a puddle of rainwater, making slight ripples that ended in a sizzling sound.

The crushed clamshell parking lot echoed Bobby's steps as he casually strolled to his prized Corvette. He paused for a moment, admiring the vehicle. "Will you look at that fuckin' car? What a beauty! I love this thing!"

Don chose Bobby's moment of distraction to make his move. He stepped around the tree with the bat already cocked over his shoulder. Three quick paces, and then he crossed his legs as if he were stepping into a fastball pitch. The bat flashed like aluminum lightening, catching Bobby squarely on the back of his skull with a deafening clang.

Bobby heard the crack as he was hurled toward his shiny red car, landing on the hood with a thud. One of Bobby's favorite ways to intimidate others was to walk up face-to-face and touch the other person's nose with his nose. Then he would slap them into submission before they knew what had happened. This time it was Bobby touching his nose to his own reflection in the polished finish of his taffy-apple Corvette.

Don stood behind Bobby as he lay across the hood. His peripheral vision caught the butt of a gun protruding from under Bobby's shirt, so he retrieved the 9mm Glock from the holster on Bobby's right hip. A strange feeling came over Don. Anxiety disappeared as anger filled his body. "Hey, what the fuck were you gonna' do with this, Bobby Boo? Were you gonna' shoot me Asshole?"

Don walked around to the side of the car. He grabbed a fistful of Bobby's hair, lifting his bleeding head. "Hey Bobby Boo, I said what the fuck were you gonna' do with this?" In a teasing childish tone, he taunted, "Were ya' gonna' shoot me, asshole?"

Bobby tried to speak, but he could only make gurgling sounds as blood gushed out of his nostrils and mouth. In his mind, he screamed, *You son of a bitch, I am going to kill you! I'm gonna' break you up real bad this time, Baby!*

But all Don could hear was incoherent gurgling. His anger shifted into ninth gear as adrenaline raced through his body. With Bobby down, something clicked. He became even more aggressive. He was going to teach this bully bouncer a lesson he would never forget, if he survived.

Don took up his position behind his prey once again. Bobby's fat ass was showing above his belt. Don slid the gun into the waistband of his own pants. Then he raised the bat in his right hand, lifting it high over his right shoulder. "I'm going to beat you like a baby harp seal."

The bat hung suspended for a moment and then flew down with menacing speed, catching Bobby on the right temple. The bat felt like it had sliced through warm butter. It continued past the target and followed through until it stopped in mid-air over Don's left shoulder. He felt like he was at the plate and had just made a homerun out of the park.

Bobby did not feel any pain, but he had immediate sensations of nausea and vertigo. Meanwhile, his left eye could not focus. Images seemed to turn upside down without him moving his head. Don swung the weapon again, left to right, catching the left temple of Bobby's head this time.

Bobby flashed back in time, seeing his father standing over him after giving him a fierce beating. He cried out in his mind, *Please Dad ... don't ... don't hit me again ... please ... don't!*

Don screamed out, "You no good dirty son of a bitch!" Don's eyes bulged out of their sockets as he lifted the bat high over his head. "You ain't never ever gonna' pick on me again!"

Don swung down with intense force; bone and brain spattered the hood and windshield. Bobby died, releasing his grip on a heavy satchel in his right hand that he'd held onto throughout the attack. Don heard it drop to the ground. A moment later Bobby followed the satchel, sliding off the hood like a two hundred and fifty pound bag of potatoes. Don wisecracked, "Hey Bobby, what did you drop there?"

Don picked up the satchel and placed it on the blood-spattered hood. Placing his thumbs on each release, he pressed and the locks popped open at the same time with a double snap. Lifting the cover, he exposed a stash of cash neatly lined up and bundled into one thousand dollar increments. Don gave a long whistle as he feasted his eyes on the dead presidents. He closed the valise, placing it on the ground next to Bobby's body. With an evil smile, Don said, "I know ... I'll make it look like a robbery!"

He unbuckled Bobby's belt and removed the holster, placing it on his own hip along with the Glock. He then emptied all of Bobby's pockets inside out. He found a wad of big bills and put it into his own pocket.

Don said, "Roll over, you fat fuckin' pig," as he pulled hard on Bobby's arm to flip him onto his stomach. He ripped the back pocket, removing the wallet. He rifled through it, finding a driver's license, a Blue Cross card Bobby would no longer need, and a photo unmistakably of Bobby with a woman when he was a little boy.

"Hey Bobby Boo, who is this?" Don continued in a child's voice. "Is this you and your mommy?"

Then in a deep evil voice, he yelled, "Well, fuck you and your mommy!" With that, he dumped all of the contents of the wallet on the ground.

Don picked up the bloody bat and used Bobby's shirt to wipe it clean. Recovering the valise and bat, he walked nonchalantly past the front door of the club, making a beeline toward his truck parked at the mall across the highway. He strolled, taking his time as if he were walking down Tremont Street on a sunny Sunday afternoon. No one was out at this time of the morning. When he got to his truck, he tossed the valise to the other side of the seat. He slid into the truck and lit up a Camel. "That wasn't so tough. Shit, I could do that every night and not even break a sweat."

Don looked back across the highway at the corpse lying on the ground. In a loud voice he called out, "Hey Bobby, you fat ass prick ..." Then he chuckled, "You ain't gonna' feel so good in the fuckin' mornin', you cocksucker! You got just what you deserved – YOU'S DEAD!"

Don shifted the truck into gear and drove off whistling, "Who's Afraid of the Big Bad Wolf." Then he burst out in a high tenor voice, "Who's afraid of the big bad wolf, the big bad wolf, the big bad wolf? Who is afraid of the big bad wolf? Noooooooot meeeeeeeeeeeeee! Ha, ha, ha, ha!"

Twenty Nine

Amanda

Still feeling the rush of power from killing Bobby, Don drove around in the wee hours and into the next afternoon.

Don put Bobby in his place – where he thought he belonged – in the ground. Each time he got away with doing something bad without suffering repercussions, he grew more emboldened. He wasn't born a thief, kidnapper, or rapist, and now a murderer – but he morphed into being one over time. He did not feel anything when he did something against the rules and regulations of society: no conscience, no guilt, and no crime. This lack of empathy would become a great tool in his arsenal in the not-too-distant future, when his career in crime would escalate.

His victory over Bobby, someone who was an evil bully in and of himself, had opened the door for a vicious killer. Don would never be pushed around anymore by anyone. Fear of the law, or of punishment from a supreme creator, no longer existed in his mind. He grabbed the power because it was there for the taking.

Don got high from the euphoria of the power that came from taking advantage of his weaker brethren. The pickings were easy and there for the taking, as any wise guy knew.

Brute force was all it took. Conscience was a thing of childhood and only for those fearful of taking the future into their own hands. To be successful, Don knew he had to be brutal, without pity or emotion.

Getting out of his truck for a walk in the afternoon, he eventually found himself standing in front of a provocative clothing store. They had live models who were modeling the store's fashions in the front display window. Some wore short skirts above the knee while others had on miniskirts. One thing they had in common – all the girls were to kill for. They all had chiseled figures with tight asses and firm tits with big nipples. One model was trying to stare Don down.

That broad is givin' me the eye. I know when someone locks eyes with me, I got a chance, especially when neither one of us looks away. Each of them was thinking the same thing. *I like what I see, and I see what I like.*

There was a magnetism they transferred with just a look – a desire – a thought that traveled from one mind to another and everything was understood. She mouthed the words, "Come inside, I want you!"

Don found himself walking through the automatic doors. The aroma of cheap but sensual perfume filled the air. The model opened the partition of the display window as she stepped down.

"Hi, I'm Amanda," she spoke with a soft, sweet, gentle voice. Her eyes had just the right amount of liner. Her lips were just a little puffy with deep cherry lipstick framed by a pink liner. Her arms and legs looked like pink velvet, soft and natural to the touch. *Man, I'd love to taste this sweet morsel of meat.*

"Can I help you to choose something for that special someone? I can put together an outfit that she will really love."

"Shh-ure," Don said as he raised his right eyebrow, giving her a seductive look.

"I've got flavored edible underwear – apple, grape, or orange – you could get all three."

"Great, I'll take them."

"What a surprise for her. I guarantee they will really turn her on."

He started blushing slightly. Amanda read his body language, and it turned her on. She felt the same attraction.

"Give me two pair of everything up to five hundred bucks worth in your size. Put each set of the clothes into two separate bags." He reached into his pocket and counted out five one-hundred dollar bills. Placing the cash in Amanda's hand he asked, "What time do you get off work?"

Amanda parted her lips slightly, showing she had perfect pearly whites. Slowly a smile crossed her face, "Are you asking me out on a date?"

"Yea ... Yeah, I am!"

Amanda gave a half giggle, "What's your name?"

"Don ... Don Ricci."

"Well Don, I get off at nine tonight."

And I'll be getting off after that, Don thought. "I'll be here at eight forty-five."

"It will just take about a half hour to help you choose the right outfits."

"No, no ... you choose the outfits. I want two matching groups of clothes. I'll buy one for you, and the other I'll take home."

Amanda squealed, "Oh my God, for me? Are you tryin' to win my heart?"

Don smiled and Amanda said, "If so, you're doing a good job. I get a store discount, you know."

"Good, that's just what I want to hear. See you tonight." He walked out the door, giving a low growl that Amanda heard.

She smiled, "Oh I think I'm gonna' have some real fun tonight with a ... tall ... dark ... handsome ... stranger! Oooooh, purrrrrrrrrr!"

Thirty

Amanda in the Yacht

Don took a lengthy walk along the Charles River. The Harvard Sculling Crew looked sharp as always as they cut the water with pulsating strokes; each time the boat would jump ahead with the power from the oars.

In no time, he crossed by way of Charles Street Bridge to the M.I.T. side of Cambridge. Turning right, he walked for two more miles. Passing by the private yacht clubs, he thought, *I oughta' buy a boat and join one of these clubs. I bet I'd meet elegant, foxy ladies. I can see myself leaning against the boat rail with a crystal glass full of booze! There, lounging in a deck chair would be this good lookin' head.*

He stopped and studied the distinct lack of security on the docks. He thought, *Hey, wait a minute. Wouldn't it be cool to bring Amanda back here? I just might do that! I'll tell her that I own that big boy right there."*

The stern bore the name "The Queen Ann." He had picked the biggest yacht on the river. *What the hell – she'll never know.*

Don tried to look nonchalant, pretending he was just observing traffic, as he made sure all was clear and safe.

Walking through the unlocked gate, he proceeded onto the dock and up the gangplank. Standing at the boat's railing for a moment, he knocked five times in quick succession on the hull. The only thing he heard was the irate drivers tooting their horns in traffic.

Don stepped onto the deck and walked aft. The wheel was made of the finest mahogany. Don stood behind it, placing his hands on the pegs. His imagination took over as he saw himself sailing down the river, out into the Atlantic, and all the way to the south sea islands of the Pacific.

The cabin door had a padlock securing it. Biting his lip, he searched for something to pop the lock. He found a screwdriver in a miniature toolbox that was attached to the sidewall of the cabin. Reaching in, he found just the right size tool. *Awfully considerate of the owner to leave this here to help me out.*

He slipped it through the loop of the lock, pulling hard. There was a crunching sound as the old screws attaching the latch plate to the boat lost their bite, slid out, and released the bulkhead door.

Walking down the stairs and into the galley, he strained his eyes. There sitting on the table was a gallon-size candle with a huge wick. Don took out a Camel cigarette, lit it, and then lit the wick. He took a deep drag, exhaling the smoke through his nose. The wick took hold and warmed the room with a yellowish hue. He closed the curtains over the portholes. *Hey, this is nice ... real nice! I wonder if there's any booze.*

Opening a cabinet over the chart desk, he found a bottle of 30-year-old Glenfiddich single malt scotch. "Perfect!"

Sitting on the bunk, he kicked back, fantasizing about Amanda. Closing his eyes for a moment, he fell asleep.

Then the chimes from the clock struck eight bells, jarring him awake.

"Shit, I gotta' get goin' if I'm to be back by nine." He glanced over to the table and thought, *I'll just leave the candle lit since we'll be back within two hours. Besides, if there is a fire ...* He finished out loud, "Ha, no skin off my nose!"

Don passed the Museum of Science on the Charles. It brought back memories of the days when his father was still living. George Ricci would explain all of the displays to curious little Donny. He smiled when he thought of the musical stairs that played songs when he and other kids ran up and down at breakneck speeds.

At 8:45 sharp, Don leaned against the store window. Amanda walked out carrying two large bags. She wore an ear-to-ear smile, red blouse, black skirt, high heels, and looked damn good.

"Hi there, how you doin'? Have you been waiting long?"

"No, I just got here. I told you I'd be back at 8:45. How was your day?"

"Oh God, it was dead as nails. You were my only sale today."

"Well it was a good one, though, and you get to keep half the clothes."

She said with a foxy giggle, "That's true, thank you ... that's so nice of you to do, really. Where are we goin'?"

"I thought we could walk over to my yacht on the Charles and have a drink."

Amanda was a good-looking woman but not much in the brain department. "Oh, God, did you say your yacht? Are you rich? I mean, do you have money? I mean, really, I can't believe it ... you have a yacht?"

Amanda took over the conversation, talking all of the way to the river. Because of her lengthy recitation, Don felt like he had known her for years. She started telling him about when she was born, about her family, her schools, her likes and dislikes. Don was relieved when they finally stepped onboard.

"Don, oh my God! This is yours? Oh my, I love your boat!"

"It's a yacht – not a boat." Don led the way to the galley, sliding the door open.

Amanda giggled as she teetered down each step with nervous anticipation. The candle gave the room a sensuous atmosphere. Wide-eyed, Amanda spun around, looking at her surroundings.

"Now, this is what I really call living!" She put the bags down on the table. Turning to Don, she took his face in her hands and kissed his lips. She continued until he responded and kissed her in return.

Don said, "We should have a drink to our new friendship."

"Yeaaaah – what you got?"

"Imported Scotch … nothing but the best."

He reached for the bottle, pouring a three-fingered glass for each of them. Don raised his glass but Amanda stopped him before he could make a toast.

"Wait, wait … let me change first!" She grabbed one of the bags and stepped into the head, closing the door. From behind the door she called, "It'll only take a second."

True to her word, she stepped out wearing only bright red, apple-flavored underpants. "There you go … how do like these apples?"

Don smiled approvingly.

She stepped forward, unlatched his belt, and pulled it off his pants. She then pulled his zipper slowly and bent down, holding his pants as he stepped aside. She was eye level and could see he was excited. She pulled his underwear down as if he was a stripper, teasing him.

Amanda parted her lips and mouthed him gently. Doing this shot signals throughout Don's body, and a moan escaped his lips. She put her hands on each cheek and pulled him towards her, forcing him deep into her throat.

After a time Amanda stood up and unbuttoned Don's shirt, peeling it off him slowly. He let Amanda be in complete control. He was there for the pure enjoyment of the experience and could tell she knew how to please a man. "Don, lie down on the bed face down," she whispered.

He did as she requested. Reaching into her bag, she took out hand cream, squirting a liberal amount into her hand. She rubbed her hands together, warming the lotion to her body temperature. Slowly, she applied the lubricant over his shoulders. This was when she noticed the fresh scars on his back.

In a sorrowful tone she asked, "Oh, Don Baby, what happened to your back?"

Don thought for a moment and answered, "I was stabbed by a jealous husband while I was fucking his wife."

She gasped, "Oh my God, did he come home and catch you in the act?"

"I'd rather not talk about it, thank you."

"Oh, sorry." She continued until she had massaged and relaxed every muscle in his back, legs, and feet. He turned over and sat up on the bed.

Amanda reached for her glass. Taking a sip, she brought the glass between her breasts and bowed her head slightly. She asked, "Do I make you happy, Don?"

It was four in the morning when Amanda opened her eyes. Don was still asleep, breathing heavily after having had sex with her for hours. The candlelight enhanced Don's features. She sat up in the corner, crossed her legs and admired every inch of his body from his feet to the thick hair on his head.

His chest moved rhythmically with each powerful breath. He was now limp but still ample. She watched as his testicles moved ever so slowly. They rose and dropped in a rhythm that excited her even more. She spread her thighs and masturbated, staring directly at Don's penis. She climaxed with a moan.

Don opened his eyes, "What a vision of loveliness you are."

Amanda kept massaging herself as Don became erect once again. He reached for her feet; grabbing her ankles, he pulled her slowly toward him. She spread her legs, knees up, open to him as he slid so effortlessly into her open, welcoming arms.

The sun was just rising over Bunker Hill as they prepared to leave. Hand in hand, they walked down the dock and onto solid ground.

Amanda smiled and said, "Don, you really know how to rock a woman's boat! When will I see you again?"

Don did not answer but smirked at the compliment, returning her sensual gaze. They walked to the Charles River Subway on the Cambridge side. Again, while they walked, Amanda ruled the conversation.

By the time they stepped onto the train, Don knew everything about her and then some. She told about her mother, father, brothers, sisters, aunts, and uncles. She had worked at the Assembly Mall as a kid. When she graduated from Somerville High, she took a class in modeling and then went to work at the adult toy store.

They disembarked at Park Street Station. Amanda and Don stood on the platform as passengers packed into the cars. The last one had to duck down and slide under someone's arm before the doors closed.

Amanda said, "Don, do I talk too much, really, do I? Do I talk too much … for you?"

"No … not at all, I'm a good listener, really."

"When I asked you when I would see you again, you didn't answer."

"Well, I don't know. Um … do you want to go out … next … ah … week? Give me your phone number, and I'll call you."

"Sure!" Pulling a slip of paper from her purse, she wrote her number down. "Don, do you want to walk me home? I'm just down the street, and besides, you will know where to pick me up next week."

Don really did not want to go to her house. He had played the game, and now he just wanted to leave. He didn't have any plans, with or without Amanda, for the time being. She might be a one-night stand, or she might not.

He gave in, and they were at her door in fifteen minutes. She lived on the fringe of China Town. The smells of the foods and spices floated in the morning air, and they really were not appetizing at this time of day. They stopped at a three-story brownstone that had seen better days. Chinese letter graffiti was spray painted over the front wall in gang-related symbols.

"Come on up; I'll make you some breakfast. I bet you're hungry. Do you want some bacon and eggs? I make a mean cup of coffee."

Don heard the right words. He hadn't eaten anything, other than Amanda's candy underwear, since yesterday when he had his little business meeting with the bum. Those two burgers were a distant memory.

"Yeah ... yeah, that would fill the bill. I would like that just fine."

Amanda smiled with joy, and they both shuffled up to the third floor in nothing flat. She slipped the key into the bolt lock and turned it with a loud click. The apartment was just one large room that served as living quarters. Off of that, there was a small galley kitchen with a tiny fridge and stove. The shades were rolled up, and there was a perfect view from every window of the crowded Southeast Expressway. You could see into every car as it passed by. Below the window and closer to the street, Chinese businessmen ran their shops the same way they would if they were living in Beijing. People were huddled around the bus stop waiting for the MTA bus to take them downtown.

Don smelled the aroma of bacon frying in a pan and then he heard the crack and the sizzle of raw eggs hitting the hot grease. "Don Honey, do you want grape jelly or strawberry jam on your English muffins?"

"Grape is fine ... sure smells good. To tell you the truth, I haven't been thinking of food much since I met you yesterday."

Amanda thought to herself, *Well that's nice ... that makes two of us then!*

Breakfast was drawn out as Don told Amanda some truths and non-truths. On the whole, he held back most of his thoughts. He made up stories about his dad. The life story he told her was what he wished had happened to him as a young boy living at home with an intact family.

"Well, I got to go. I'll see you later. Thanks for the breakfast. You were goin' to work today?"

"Yeah, but not until four this afternoon. You want to stay until I got to go to work?"

"No, I got to go."

Don got up, grabbed his jacket off the coat hook, swung it over his broad shoulder, and picked up the second bag of clothing. Amanda got a chill down her back. *It's so sexy the way he moves with so much authority. Oh my God, he stands there like a Greek god or something.*

Amanda moved against his body, reached up, and kissed him once more. She gave him a long, wet one to remind him where he could be satisfied in his time of need. Reaching down, he cupped her ass by each cheek, giving her a very firm hold and almost lifting her off of the floor. It took her breath away.

Closing the door, Amanda heard his footsteps fade away as he traversed the stairs. She rushed to the window and watched him take long strides as he disappeared from view, moving faster than the other people walking on the sidewalk. Once in a while, he would step off the curb, then on again, pressing past the crowd. She turned away and looked at her humble abode. "He has so much, and I have so little."

Her eyes filled with tears as she wondered if she would ever see him again. She suddenly realized he had her number but he hadn't given her his. She swallowed hard, "Well, I guess we'll see."

Thirty One

The Escape

It was Labor Day and forty-eight hours since Don scored a home run on Bobby's head. He hadn't been home, and Julie noticed it had been quiet upstairs for quite some time.

Julie had lost a lot of weight. She was now very skinny because of Don's forced diet, as well as from the extreme stress of living in captivity. Sitting on the bed with a pillow behind her for a cushion, her eyes closed as she fantasized about what it would be like to bite into a sweet, crisp, flaky honey-filled baklava with crunchy walnuts. Her legs were pulled close to her chest where her chin was resting on her knees. Opening her eyes, suddenly she came back to the present, looking directly at the bars.

She thought, *That's funny, they look as if they have moved. I could swear they're wider than before.* She got up, walked over to the bars, and bent her neck, moving forward. To her surprise, her head slipped past them with a very snug fit. Looking around, she craned her neck.

"So this is what it feels like to be on the outside."

Carefully, she maneuvered her bony head back into the cell. She removed the nightgown the Master insisted that she wear when it was evening. She would put it on when the single, dingy stream of daylight was not coming through the coal chute window. Opening the mini-fridge, she took out a bottle of Italian salad dressing and examined the label. "I bet this will work," she said.

Pouring a liberal amount into her left hand, she gasped from the chill of the cool liquid as she applied it to her right breast and up over her shoulder as goose bumps popped up. She continued rubbing with both hands as if she was soaping herself down in the shower. The slippery fluid spread easily over the back of her neck, face, and torso as she smoothed it all over her body.

She whispered, "If it works, it works. Now is the time to escape, before that son of a bitch comes back. If I can't get past the bars, I will just shower off, and he'll never know."

Her pulse raced as she slipped one leg between the bars and stepped off of the cell's carpet onto the cool cement floor outside. The rib cage posed her greatest difficulty. Julie exhaled fully and then slid through and away from the bars, her backside hanging up just a bit. She was past the bars quickly and stood there, looking at the enclosure for a moment, before reaching past the bars to the floor inside the cage, retrieving the nightgown.

It was not easy to get the gown to cover her body because of the greasy, exotic Italian perfume she had donned. She smelled like the new salad kid in the kitchen of the busiest restaurant in town.

Quietly, she opened the small basement window that had been a coal chute in bygone years, located near the ceiling. Piling anything she could find to help her climb up to the window, she slithered out the opening but ripped her nighty on an old, rusty nail. She found herself standing semi-naked in the fresh air. Only then did she realize just how stale, foul, and dank the air had been in the basement.

Julie closed her eyes and inhaled deeply. When she opened them, the darkness of the night disappeared with the brightness of the starlit sky. *Freedom ... I've finally gotten ... free!*

Julie kept low, creeping in the shadows, hidden from view. She muttered, "I don't know where I'm going or where I am, but at least I'm free."

Survival and escape were the only things that concerned Julie. It's surprising what people will do when they must.

Fear kept her going despite her exhaustion; fear that when he saw her missing he would come after her with vengeance because she had the audacity to spurn him. She began running in blind terror.

In a low whisper that only she could hear, she prayed, "God, I know he's going to get me. He'll capture me and torture me again, good God, Holy Father, don't let this happen to me."

Thirty Two

Hi Honey, I'm Home

Don descended the creaking stairs, putting on the lights with a loud click. Now that he had gotten his confidence back by taking revenge on Bobby, thoughts of lust and ecstatic orgasms swirled in his head. He figured it was time to try approaching Julie again. He thought the bag of cunnilingus candy might be just the right peace offering, since he'd bought it from Amanda anyway.

"Julie Baby, I'm gonna' give you such a hard fuck you're going to pass out." He continued half-jokingly, "Do you want to eat some pizza first, or do you want to get down to business now?"

Walking over to the bars, Don peered at the cot in the shadows. He strained his eyes, and panic set in as he dropped the bag of candy underwear. He screamed, "Oooooh fffuck!"

He raced to retrieve the cell keys he kept on the far wall. Unlocking his private Garden of Eden, he charged in only to find it empty. Loneliness and despair set in for his loss. "Oh shit, where is she? How the hell did she get out? Doesn't she realize how much I love her? I mean, look at all I've done for her. What do I do now?"

As he stood there, despair seethed into anger, "She is just a fuckin' bitch, a no good fuckin' bitch. She doesn't know what she's doing to me, that BITCH!"

He sat on the cot, pondering his loss of all that could have been. "I love her so much … hadn't I shown her how much I care? But she didn't return any of the emotions draining out of my soul. Hadn't I helped her change? Didn't I give her a new body? She had it hidden under all of that fat. I made her what she is now. Why would she desert me when we had both achieved so much together?"

He reached over and grabbed the wedding dress. Pulling it toward him hard, it made a tearing sound before coming off the heavy hanger. He cradled it tenderly in his arms as he spoke sadly to it. "Oh Baby, where are you? Why have you left me? I love you so much."

Don sat there, rocking back and forth, then he screamed and ripped the front of the dress from the back. Standing, he raised both pieces over his head and screamed, "You fuckin' bastard, Julie! You ungrateful son of a bitch! I shoulda' killed you when I had the chance!"

Throwing the scraps of the torn wedding dress on the floor, he stomped on them as if he were killing an adversary. Exhausted from his rage, he collapsed to the floor, moaning. Devastated and alone, he said, "Now what the fuck am I gonna' do? The cops will be coming here to arrest me. I'm not going to jail. Screw them – they aren't going to get me – I'll kill them all!"

Pondering just what his next move would be, he stepped over to the table and picked up the cord from the wedding dress box. "They're not going to get me," he said.

He fashioned a hangman's knot out of the cord. Attaching it to the rafter above, he slipped the noose over his head and tightened it by bending his knees. It tightened quickly with his weight. His eyes became bloodshot as vessels broke one after another. The cord slid easily, tightening, closing the loop around his neck, which constricted his carotid artery.

Don felt so surreal and cold ... then darkness, loss of consciousness ... his body jerked and twisted in its death roll. An involuntary spasm shot into Don's strong legs. It propelled him into the air, and he came down with such dead weight force the cord snapped loudly like a violin string.

His body lay quiet, not moving, but robbing the Reaper of his quest, Don suddenly let out a loud gasp, and then another. Feebly, he reached for his neck, digging his fingernails into his skin and removing what was left of the broken cord.

He was back – from where he did not know. He only knew he was relieved to be back from the dead, even though among the living he felt so helpless and alone. Lying on top of the shredded wedding dress, he curled into a fetal position. His eyes welled up and tears flowed as he broke down, weeping as if he was a child once again.

Thirty Three

Finding Julie

After running for what seemed like hours, Julie's legs began to fatigue. She could run no further, and she dropped into some high grass by the roadway. Panting and exhausted, Julie tried to hold her breath so she could listen for the sound of her captor pursuing her.

It was Labor Day weekend, and Officer Joe O'Malley was making his rounds on patrol just before crashing for the shift. It was a common practice in most police departments and encouraged by brass who had once found themselves unfortunate enough to pull the midnight shift. Joe slipped down a dirt road past an overgrown apple orchard and parked the cruiser in the dark. In this out-of-the-way location, he would escape notice from anyone and could "go under" until sun up.

The words of his commanding officer, Sergeant O'Toole, still haunted him, "I don't wanna' hear from anybody unless it's a fuckin' murder."

If you disturbed the shift commander from his slumber, you were screwed, and you would find yourself walking the beat, hand-checking doors.

Julie had lain in the grass for hours when the cruiser came down the road and stopped not thirty feet from where she was hiding. The engine cut off and all grew quiet but for the crickets and the swarm of mosquitoes feasting on her near-naked body.

Oh, it's him ... I know it. She closed her eyes and prayed to God the All Mighty to save her from this deranged person. Memories flashed in her mind of the last months of her life, of the emotional and physical torment. She started to shake uncontrollably, knowing he could hear every sound she made.

I can feel him ... he's going to get me. I know he's going to get me. I know it. I can sense his eyes on me right now.

Finally, after an hour in prayer, Julie took control of her emotions and peered in the direction of the car. She was dumbfounded when she saw an emblem lit up by starlight. The letters glowing on the passenger door read, "Town of Griffin Police."

O'Malley had his eyes closed, breathing deeply, and falling into REM sleep when there was a tapping on the door to his right. Jumping up in fear from the sudden noise, he experienced an adrenaline rush. In a single fluid motion, he drew his revolver, cocked the hammer, and pointed it into the face of the phantom banshee.

Emotions flowed from every part of her body and soul. "Help, help me, please, for God's sake, help me ... he's after me, please help!"

Joe yelled, "Don't move! I will blow your fuckin' head off." Then his brain registered the disheveled creature in distress, and he lowered the gun from her face. Gently easing the hammer down into a half-cock position, he slid the firearm back into the breakfront holster to sleep in comfort once again.

She had difficulty standing and slowly collapsed from view. Jumping out of the cruiser, Joe flooded the area with his Mag-lite. Crouching on the ground, sobbing, was a woman in the shreds of a nightgown.

"Help me please!"

Joe knelt down and reached out to her. He touched her arm and felt something moist. Joe sensed she was just sweating from being in shock. Then he became aware of the overpowering aroma of his favorite salad dressing. He had reached out to comfort her, and it was too late to back off as he looked down at his pristine blue shirt. It had sucked up the oils as if it were a sponge.

Even though he was in full uniform and in a marked cruiser, she called out. "Call the police, please, call the police."

"I am the police. I'm Officer O'Malley. You're safe ... no one is going to hurt you. It's okay now, it's okay! Are you all right? Are you hurt at all?"

"He's after me," she whispered.

"Who is after you?"

She whispered again, and Joe had difficulty hearing, "Him ... the Master guy ... he stole me and locked me up in the basement. He's coming, he's coming after me."

Joe quickly stood up and held his Maglite far to his left, scanning the area. Seeing nothing, he bent down to the woman once again. "I don't see anyone out there. You're safe with me now. Let me get you some help."

Joe reached to the radio microphone attached to the left shoulder of his shirt. Holding the mike, his finger slipped off the button from the oily dressing on his hand. Wiping it onto his pants leg, he tried once again. In a modulated voice he said, "This is car four. I need an ambulance down here at the old dirt road going to the Brown's Apple Farm. I have a woman who seems to be disoriented and in need of medical attention."

The dispatcher barked back, "10-4, I got one on the way."

The lieutenant and a private from the fire department had been on duty since four that afternoon. The keys were in the ignition of the ambulance, and it started without hesitation. The driver pulled the switch on the strobe lights, and they flashed to life. The lieutenant jumped into the passenger seat, grabbed the radio from the cradle charger, and called out excitedly, "Dispatch, wha'cha got?"

"Hey Lou, I got a call from O'Malley. He's on the dirt road goin' out to the old Brown's Apple Farm."

"10-4." The lieutenant changed channels to the cruiser band, "Car four, pickup ... Joe, can you hear me? Where are ya'? Wha'cha got."

Wiping his hand once again on his pants, he reached for the button on his mic. "I'm on the dirt road at Brown's Apple Farm right where the trees start. I have a woman here who needs medical attention."

The lieutenant shot back, "Is she conscious?"

"Yeah, but she appears to be a little confused and agitated."

"10-4, I'll be right there."

Julie started to cry uncontrollably, "Oh God, thank you for answering my prayers."

Joe had difficulty understanding what she was saying as she babbled on. "It's okay, Miss, you're safe now. I have an ambulance on the way."

Wild-eyed, she grabbed his arm. Joe considered himself manly, but when she grabbed him, it felt like a pneumatic vice. He winced at the pain from her grip. "You have to protect me. He's coming ... he's coming after me!"

He pulled his arm back and took her hand in his. Joe said in a confident voice, "I will check all of the area as soon as the ambulance gets here. No one is going to bother you, don't worry. What's your name, Miss?"

Julie looked up into Joe's eyes and said nothing.

"It's okay, it's okay, what is your name?"

Julie lowered her head and said with a deep sob, "My name is ... Julie Booker."

Stunned, Joe replied, "Ms. Booker ... I've been looking for you for months. I've finally found you!"

Julie looked back into Joe's face with disbelief, "You've been looking for me? Oh God, I thought I was lost forever. You were looking for me? I wish I'd known. I'd lost faith that I would ever be free again!"

"Who kidnapped you?

She replied weakly, "I don't know."

"Where were you being held?"

"I don't know. I don't know ... I DON'T KNOW!" Suddenly, she broke down again. Julie wrapped her arms around Joe's neck as if he were her daddy, seeking comfort and consoling.

He held her and muttered to himself, "What's taking them so long to get here?"

In the distance, they heard the wailing sirens. Joe held her close and rocked her as if she was his child, while he kept an alert eye on the dark orchard. Straining to see the lights, the flickering strobes finally came into view. Joe had on his interior lights with both front doors wide open as well as the emergency lights flashing on the roof.

The ambulance driver slammed on the brakes, sliding on the gravel road up to the cruiser. A dust cloud rose but was blown away by the gentle breeze of the night. Flinging open the back doors, the lieutenant grabbed the medical kit. Running at top speed, he slipped on the wet grass and went down with a thud, landing on a flat rock. He picked himself up and limped with pain to the victim cradled in Joe's arms.

The lieutenant grabbed the blood pressure cuff from the bag. Taking a reading, Julie's blood pressure was 220 over 95 – not surprising since she was hysterical.

The driver carried over a stretcher for Julie."Okay Miss, let me help you."

"Yes ... please. All of a sudden, I feel so weak and tired. What's wrong with me?"

"Miss, you're in emotional shock, but you'll be okay. Let's get you to the hospital and get you checked up."

"Thank you ... yes ... yes, please take me to the hospital." She seemed to drift off to sleep, but then fought to stay awake because she did not want to wake up and find her escape was but a dream. At the hospital, they gave her a thorough examination. To no one's surprise, she was in poor physical condition due to the loss of so much weight so quickly.

Thirty Four

The Hospital

The Chief read Patrolmen O'Malley's report and then gave it to Detective Jeff Miller the next morning, which prompted Jeff to go immediately to the hospital. He flashed his gold badge to the information desk receptionist. "Hi, I'm Detective Miller. What room is Julie Booker in? She was admitted early this morning."

The way the detective spoke, it was not a question but a demand. The operator gave him an annoyed look, and then her fingers danced on her keyboard. She spoke in a direct tone, "Julie Booker is on the third floor, Room 3C."

Jeff impatiently stood waiting for the elevator as he repeatedly pressed the button. Joe O'Malley walked up to him, "Hey Jeff, I see you got my report."

"Oh yeah, yeah ... I got it ... ahh ... this morning when I got to the station. How come you didn't call me last night?"

"I didn't think it was necessary to bother you. After all, you were sound asleep. Besides, this was something I was involved in from the beginning, and I wanted to finish it myself."

Before Jeff could reply, the elevator door opened. A shapely nurse looked up, smiling as the two policemen stepped into the elevator. The nurse spoke up, "Hi Jeff, so wonderful to see you. Where have you been all these years?"

She turned to Joe, "This is my Jeff – my old boyfriend from college days." With that, she stepped up and kissed Jeff on the lips. A flustered and embarrassed Jeff found himself at an uncharacteristic loss for words. "Uh ... Hi, how are you doin'?"

She reached up, touching his cheek with the palm of her hand. "How did I ever let you get away from me?"

Joe smirked and reached over, pushing the call button to send the elevator to the basement. He stepped out as the door closed, leaving Jeff to fend for himself with his old flame. He went directly to Room 3C. The door was ajar about six inches; he stopped and listened to the conversation within.

Ten minutes earlier, the hospital psychiatrist had come to Julie's room. She was already awake and looking out the window in a trance when the doctor arrived. Julie heard a knock at the door. Turning, she observed a well-dressed man with rimless glasses. His eyewear distracted her.

He extended his hand, "Hello, I'm Doctor Berger, the resident psychiatrist. I understand you have gone through a harrowing experience. Would you care to talk about it?"

Julie was still examining his glasses when she realized he was speaking to her. She came out of the trance. Tilting her head, she asked, "What ... what did you say?"

"I am Doctor Mel Berger," he said slower and more distinctly. "I am the resident psychiatrist for the hospital. I understand you have gone through a harrowing ... a traumatic ... experience. Would you care to talk about it with me?"

Julie looked directly at Burger, challenging him, "Why ... why would I want to talk about it with you? I mean ... I don't know you from a hole in the wall! You walk in here as if you were God, and I should just open up to you? As if … you were the Master? Well, you're not ... and I don't care to talk about anything!"

"The Master, that's curious. What do you mean when you say 'The Master'?"

"Him, he wanted me to always call him Master."

"Was this a way of controlling you? Making you call him Master?"

"I guess so. He did control me most of the time."

Dr. Berger scribbled a few notes, "Julie, I can understand your hesitancy to talk to me, really I can. Do you now feel more relaxed? I'll give you some time to think about it. May I come back to see you tomorrow? Is that okay?"

"No," she sighed, "you can stay." She continued, "I guess I can talk more about it. I just don't know who to trust."

She mumbled and appeared to be grinding her teeth in thought. Slowly, she turned away, looking out into the sunshine once again. "I just love the sunlight ... grass, trees, anything to do with nature."

It was obvious that she was trying not to answer any questions, not wanting even to think of her ordeal. She closed her eyes to face the sun, letting her skin be drenched in warmth and comfort. She needed that warmth and light.

"You know, I was in someone's cellar for so long. It was dark ... with a musty odor. I sat in a cage and ... and rotted there. All that I could think of was ... was ... was how to kill that son of a bitch. He raped me and deserved to be killed." She turned quickly, staring straight at the doctor, "I almost got him once."

Her face contorted, "I got a hook, and I put it into his back. I hit him three times with it before it got stuck, and he got away!" Her face twisted with anger, "I felt so good seeing him screaming in agony."

Having overheard the end of the exchange, Joe walked into the room. In a cheery voice, he said, "Good morning, Ms. Booker. I'm Patrolman Joe O'Malley. I have been on your case for almost six months. I'm the officer who found you last night. Do you remember me?"

Julie turned to face Joe. In an angry voice, she growled, "Why the hell did it take you so long to find me, if you were searching so diligently? If you remember, it was me who found you."

"Yeah, and that's just what I'm here to find out. Can you tell me where you were being held?"

"I can't tell you anything. I don't know where I've been. I don't know."

"Who was responsible for your kidnapping?"

"I don't know ... I never saw his face. He always had a hood-mask on."

"What's a hood-mask? You mean something like a ski mask?"

"Yeah, only that it's made of leather with a zipper down the back."

At that moment, a very irritated Detective Miller stepped into the room. "Hello, Ms. Booker, I am Detective Jeff Miller of the Griffin Police Department. I will be right back."

He turned to Joe, "Officer O'Malley, please step outside for a moment. I must speak to you about something of the utmost importance!"

Miller turned, walking out of the room, and O'Malley followed as if he were a sheep following a Judas Ram to be butchered.

After the two policemen walked out of the hospital room, Dr. Berger looked at Julie. “I am sorry, where were we when they interrupted? Kind of strange, don’t you think? I wonder what that was all about.”

Finding an empty waiting room, the detective turned, “Do you think what you did was humorous?”

Joe just smiled but didn’t say anything.

“Well it wasn’t – get the hell out of this hospital and don’t come back! I have officially taken over this case.”

“You can’t do that!”

“I just did! Now, Patrolman O’Malley! I’m ordering you to remove yourself from this hospital ... now!”

Joe leaned forward invading Jeff’s space, “We’ll see what the Chief has to say about this!”

He turned and headed to the elevators. As if on cue, the doors opened, and he stepped inside without turning around, waiting for the doors to close.

Dr. Berger and Julie were now alone, “Oh yes ... you said you caused some physical damage to the ... person ... who was holding you against your will?”

“Yes ... I got him real good, but not good enough to kill him.”

“Julie, tell me, how did that make you feel?”

“How did it make me feel? It made me feel good … real good. Well, at least at first. I thought I could kill him and escape ... but when he didn’t die, he just walked upstairs with the hook still sticking in his back. I knew I was in trouble with him. Then I got scared ‘cause I didn’t know what he was going to do!”

“Julie, what did he do when he got back?”

Detective Jeff Miller walked back into the room with a slight grin, “So sorry about that, but ...”

The shrink stopped him in mid-sentence, "Excuse me, Detective, but I am Dr. Berger, the resident psychiatrist. Ms. Booker and I are having a counseling session. Would you be so kind as to remove yourself for the time being? I need some privacy. I'll let you know when I'm finished."

Miller looked at Berger, who stood there with his arms folded in complete control. Jeff then looked into Julie's eyes, and he felt as if he were the one who was not wanted. This was a blow to his ego, his position of authority, and the law, but he backed off.

"Sorry, I guess this is a bad time. When do you want me to come back?" He continued, "Tomorrow okay, how about two in the afternoon?"

Julie just nodded. Miller backed out of the doorway and disappeared down the hall.

Thirty Five

The Interview

Joe awoke from a light, restless sleep, aware it was time to get up. He reached over with his eyes still closed and hit the alarm clock with a heavy hand before it could sound off.

He thought of Julie. *I gotta' get back up to the hospital before that asshole beats me to the punch. He can't take my case away from me! Well, then get your ass up and moving.*

He did not check in with the desk but went directly to 3C and knocked on the door as he pushed it out of the way. Sunshine flooded the freshly made bed as the housekeeping staff dusted the shiny, waxed floor.

"Where's the lady?" Joe asked, looking around the vacated room.

The old South American woman dressed in white just grimaced and shrugged her shoulders. She didn't speak English and didn't have the slightest idea of what the policeman wanted. Joe stopped at the front desk, inquiring as to the whereabouts of Julie Booker.

"She checked herself out last night. She said she wanted to go home, and that's what she did. I didn't think it was such a good idea but her friend Barbara, who came to get her, did."

Joe drove to Julie's with the determination of a bullhead ant in mortal combat. *I'm going to find out who's responsible for this kidnapping. I'll slip that guy's ass behind bars until he's too old to be of danger to anyone else.* Joe pulled over a little too quickly, and there was a loud scraping noise as his rim hit the old granite curb.

"Shit!" He got out, surveying for damage, but found none.

Julie's lawn was freshly cut, and an engine purred in the backyard. Joe walked to the rear of the house, finding a gray-haired guy riding a tractor lawnmower around as if he were riding a go-cart at the fairgrounds. The old man smiled at Joe; he stopped and turned off the engine.

"Hi there, I'm Joe O'Malley from the Griffin Police Department. Is Julie Booker home?"

"Hi Officer, I'm Julie's neighbor, Simon Brown. I saw her this mornin' with another woman walkin' up the driveway. I thought it was one of those apparitions. It looked kinda' like her, but she was so skinny. So I calls out, 'Hey, Julie, is that you? Is that really you? I thought that you were missin'! The cops are lookin' for ya.' She tells me she just got home. She just turns around, and they walked into the house."

The old man continued, "I felt bad because the lawn was looking kind of tough and not in very good condition, so I got the rider out and zip, zip, zip ... all done!"

"Are you the neighbor who woke up in the middle of the night when she was kidnapped?"

"Yeah, yeah, that was me. I told the other cop, the guy with the gold badge. I told him all that I know."

"Well, Simon, I would like you to tell me again exactly what you remember about that night."

Simon's face went blank, "Gee, I don't know. That was a long time ago! I aaah ... I aaah …"

He reached up, scratching his day-old beard. Taking a deep breath, he held it for a few seconds. Exhaling he said, "I don't remember' so good no more. Ya' know, I ... ahh ... had a little prostate problem, they did something. I don't remember' so good no more."

Joe could see the old man suffered a great deal more than just a little prostate problem. "Simon, you're really a good neighbor, and you're doing a fine job on the lawn. I want to thank you."

Simon grinned widely, showing the years had taken a toll on his teeth.

"Keep up the good job," Joe said.

Joe had a flashback. The last time he walked up these backstairs and into this house, he was investigating a missing person and had drawn his gun. That day the adrenaline pumped through his body at a fast clip.

Joe pushed the doorbell and waited. The blinds moved, and Julie peered out through the glass. "Hi, Miss Booker, I'm Officer Joe O'Malley. I wanted to ..."

Julie stopped him in mid-sentence, "I know who you are."

Joe heard a loud click as Julie unlocked the deadbolt and swung open the door. "I want to thank you for all you have done to help me. Please come in."

She looked past Joe, to Simon sitting on the lawn mower. Calling out to him, she said, "Mr. Brown, thank you! You're so kind to cut the lawn. I really appreciate your help."

Simon turned beet red and lowered his head, smiling. "That's what good neighbors are for, Miss. See you later."

He started the machine and snapped it into drive gear, steering toward home.

Barbara, Julie's superior and friend from work, was sitting at the kitchen table. "Hi, Joe, how are you doin'?"

"Hi, Barb, I'm glad to see you, how are you doin'?"

"Good, Joe. Good."

Julie offered, "Can I get you a cup of coffee, Officer?"

"Oh, that would be nice, thank you. You know, I never drank coffee before getting on the force. Now, if I don't get my fix of caffeine every day, I start to fall asleep."

"Joe, I brought Julie home but I gotta' get to work. I'll let you two talk."

Julie turned, "Barb, thank you so much for coming and driving me home."

Barbara nodded and stepped up to Julie, wrapping her arms around her and hugging her gently. "There's no rush about comin' back to work ... you take your time." Barbara kissed Julie on the cheek. "I'll see you later. I'll be back after work, as soon as I get some night clothes at home."

Barbara turned to Joe, "I'm goin' to stay over for a time until Julie feels more at ease."

"Thank you, Barb, see you tonight," Julie said.

"Goodbye, Joe, you take care," Barbara said as she walked out the door.

Julie stepped into the dining room, returning with two antique cups and saucers that had belonged to her grandmother. The cups rattled a little as she made her way back to the table.

She wore blue jeans and a t-shirt that were several sizes too large. Her extra-long belt looked like the type a clown might wear, and she had pulled her blonde hair back into a ponytail. She looked tired.

Biting the inside of her lip, she looked at Joe sitting there. As she tilted her head, her eyes started to water. "Why me?"

More tears welled at the edge of her eyelids and overflowed down her face.

Joe had not expected her emotional breakdown. He was there to ask questions, to solve the mystery, to help his case, but he wasn't prepared for this. A man's man, he usually could handle anything that came down the pike, but this made him feel inadequate. He shifted in his chair not knowing how to show sympathy. Police are not encouraged to show their feelings.

Just then, to his relief, the coffee pot boiled over. Julie turned and pulled the pot off the burner. "I'm sorry, I didn't mean to cry."

Wiping her face, she continued, "But why me, why me? I have been asking myself that question over and over."

Julie went to the pantry; she opened a cellophane-wrapped bag of white crackers and arranged them on a dish reserved for company. Joe sat there quietly, trying to figure out how he was going to start his questioning, given her fragile emotional state.

"I'm sorry, but there isn't much here since I've been ... away. I've already emptied the fridge of the spoiled food. I guess I've got to go grocery shopping."

Julie placed the platter in the center of the table and sat across from Joe. "Oh, I am sorry! I didn't even ask you how you wanted your coffee. Do you want milk? Oh ... I don't have milk, I forgot. I had to dump everything." She looked down again, "I had ... I had to dump ... everything!"

Once again, Julie broke down crying. "Officer, I'm sorry, but I am really trying to understand why all of these things happened to me. You know what the only thing was that helped me ... that kept me alive?"

Joe didn't say anything.

"At first, it was faith in God ... I knew he would not desert me. But then, as time passed and I was ... accosted, again and again, my sorrow turned to hatred. Hatred so fierce I actually tried to kill him. I ... I would lie awake at night, trying to think of some way to kill him and escape."

"Yes, I understand."

"But that's not me. That's not me at all. Normally I don't have a malicious bone in my body. Now sometimes I feel that I have deserted God or he has deserted me. Do you think that trying to kill him was sinful?"

"No, that was survival. You had all the right in the world to protect and defend yourself from violence. Don't let the politically right thing to say and do influence your right to protect yourself."

"I guess you are right, but the Old Roman Catholic guilt gets to me sometimes."

"Julie, may I please use my tape recorder so I may go over this information again at a later date?"

"Sure whatever you need to do, go ahead."

Joe pulled a small recorder from his shirt pocket, placed it on the table next to the crackers, and pushed record. "Okay, we're all set, please go on."

"I don't know how long I was there. But I lost a great deal of weight, and that was the answer to my dilemma."

She started to laugh, with the tears still washing down her face. "I guess something good came out of this anyway – I lost weight. I've been overweight all my life. No matter how I fought to lose it, I couldn't. Now look at me! I look like a clown in these clothes. I'm going shopping tomorrow to get clothes that I can fight in, maybe some army surplus. I'm going to sign up for defense class, karate, or jujitsu, and learn to protect myself. If there is ever another encounter like this, I want to be on top. He liked my hair; he would pull on it when he raped me. Joe, do you think that I should just cut it off, all off?"

This put Joe in an uncomfortable spot. He could hear the Chief asking him, "Well Joe, did you tell that woman to cut off all of her hair, to shave her head?"

"Ahh ... Julie, I don't know, maybe a little shorter. You know, shoulder length, maybe."

"God does work in strange ways."

Changing the subject, he asked, "Can you think of anything that would help me find where you were being held?"

Julie thought for a moment, "All I remember is being woken up in my bedroom with a large knife at my throat. He was very strong; he put his hand over my mouth. I had difficulty breathing from the smell of the rubber. He had latex rubber gloves on. Then I smelled something chemical. The next thing I knew, I woke up in a cage."

Joe reached down for another cracker, nibbling it as he sipped his coffee. He also listened intently, focusing on every word and description of her harrowing experience.

"When you escaped from the basement and got outside, what did the area look like? Were there buildings, like in the city, or was it like the suburbs?"

"There were smaller homes. It was an old neighborhood. All that I can remember is that I kept running and running until I couldn't run anymore. Then I lay down in the high grass, praying he wouldn't find me! The mosquitoes kept buzzing in my ears and biting me, but I was too afraid to move and make noise."

She poured herself another cup of coffee and continued, "When I saw lights from your car, I thought it was him coming after me! Then after a long time I looked up, and I made out the writing on the side of the car in big letters that said *POLICE.* That's all I can tell you about that night."

"Yes, I know about that part of the night. It was me who found you."

"Yes, I know, but I don't remember much about that night. Except, I do remember you. I remember the lights ... the siren, and wishing they would turn that damn thing off. The doctor and the nurses were very kind. They gave me a full physical examination to see what damage might have happened, as well as checking to see if ... I was, " she shuttered, " ... pregnant."

She continued, "Everything was negative. They said I was anemic from the weight loss, but otherwise in good shape. Physically, at least. I wish I could just forget what happened to me!" She looked as if she would cry again.

Joe tried to distract her by handing her his card, "Ms. Booker, I promise I will do everything in my power to get this person and put him in jail for the rest of his life. You need to call me if you remember anything else you can tell me. Please don't hesitate; something you might think of as useless and of no value may be just the key to solving this case."

"Joe, I would like to learn how to fire a gun."

"That's a good idea. If more people carried guns, the bad guys would think twice before they would try to take advantage of someone. No one wants to die of 'lead poisoning.'"

"Joe, you could teach me how to shoot. Will you … please?"

"Well, I guess I could. Are you really serious? Could you kill someone? You know you don't shoot to just scare someone, to make him run away. You must shoot to kill."

"I can do it now; I already tried, remember? I never want to go through something like that again."

"Okay, we'll start tomorrow if you wish. Also, I would get a big dog – they're a good deterrent. Besides, they hear what's going on before we do. We could stop by the pound tomorrow after target practice."

"Okay, I've always wanted a dog. It would be more faithful and loving than a boyfriend. I need someone who will protect me."

Joe looked at her and thought, *I would protect you, if you gave me the chance.*

He said, "If you think of anything, call me. It may be the break I need to find him. Tomorrow we'll start by getting your fingerprints and background check with the F.B.I. for a license to carry a concealed weapon."

Julie nodded, "If I think of anything, I'll call you."

"Maybe we could go out for coffee and apple pie after shooting," Joe said.

"We'll see, I do like apple pie."

Thirty Six

The Introduction

It was a typical winter night in Boston, as another Nor'easter storm drove the sleet, stinging anyone on foot. Don turned up the collar on his three-quarter black leather jacket to cover his neck from the falling ice. Six months had passed since Julie's escape. Don had started popping uppers to cut the edge of his depression, and he was drinking and smoking more than usual, trying to quash his memories of the time he had her as his personal toy.

New Englanders are a strange breed of drivers. Even on a night like this, they move at breakneck speeds. Don stopped to light up a butt in front of a bar called Davy Jones' Locker. A van ran into a pothole, flinging the frozen slush into the air and spraying it all over Don. The change of temperature made him gasp. A second truck behind the van sent another wave flying through the air as Don leapt into the vestibule of the bar just in time to avoid the deluge.

Standing inside, Don spat the wet, extinguished butt to the floor. He stood there unable to see anything until his wide-open eyes adjusted to the dim light. The smell of booze and cigarette smoke filled the air, almost causing him to sneeze. To his left was a mahogany bar. The shelves behind the bar displayed every bottle of liquor on the market. There were only three lights on in the whole place.

The good-looking blond bartender appeared to be about forty. Her long hair was tied back into a ponytail. Don observed a dark-complexioned gentleman sporting curly, coal-black hair. He looked around seventy.

He stood there for a moment, shaking the water and ice off of his wet clothing as if he were a Labrador pup. The warmth of the bar gave him the urge to empty his bladder. "Gotta' men's room?"

The woman pointed to the rear of the barroom. A red exit sign illuminated the darkness. "It's next to the back door."

"Thanks! Some fuckin' idiot driver sprayed me from a pothole out front."

The man in the corner watched Don from the very moment he burst into the bar. He noticed Don walked like a heavy; shifting his weight with his first step as he headed for the restroom with urgency. The man with the drink looked over at the barmaid. She was already staring at him to see what his reaction would be. "Alice, who do ya' suppose sent him to come here?"

She just widened her eyes, rolling them in a circle and lifting her shoulder as if to say, "I don't know."

The old man started to get fidgety, although he didn't show it. He sucked hard on his butt and then put it out by unconsciously dropping it into his glass of whiskey. "Oh fuck. Hey Alice, gimme' another drink."

He started to think hard of just who would want to have him killed. *I bet that fucker comes out with his right hand down behind his leg, carrying a piece. If he does, I'm not gonna' ask questions, I'll just fuckin' drop him like the fuckin' piece of shit he is.*

The old man started to mumble to himself, "Coming after me, who the fuck does he think he is? I'll kill the son-of a-bitch."

The old man was getting more agitated as he sat there, contemplating his next move. "I whacked more fuckin' guys in bars when they was half smashed than anyone else. He thinks that I'm too old and not in the game anymore? He's goin' to have one fuckin' surprise when I drill him a new eye socket."

The men's room door was just a swing gate that parted; when Don walked through, it squeaked as it flipped back and forth. The stench of decomposing urine permeated the small room from the un-flushed urinal. He stood reading the graffiti and wondered if the phone number on the wall was for real: Suzy Swallows 1-781-555-5555 call any time $20.

Don started to chuckle and then burst into a full belly laugh, missing the bowl and pissing onto the floor for a moment before correcting the stream. He gave a little shake, zipped up, and turned to the sink.

He rinsed his hands with hot water since the soap dispenser was empty. Drying his hair with a handful of paper towels made him look as if he had combed it slick. Standing there, he looked at his fine lines and admired himself in the mirror. Satisfied, he twisted his lips in a bit of a smile. He rolled his shoulders and popped his neck. He did not have the slightest idea his life was in danger the moment he walked out the bathroom door.

Passing through the gate once more, the squeak of the door echoed throughout the empty bar. He noticed the click of his leather boots on the hardwood floor, reminding him of a Nazi officer in an old movie. The clicking heels made him walk more erect, assuming the role of power.

Swaggering as he headed back, he tried to impress the barmaid. He felt smug and cocksure because she was watching him as he came closer. What he didn't realize was she was merely anticipating what might happen next.

The old man slid his right hand to the middle of his back and gripped his revolver by its mother-of-pearl handle; he pulled back the hammer at half cock. It was held by a tight-fitting spring that would release the 38 Smith and Wesson. This was only one of five weapons he carried. In his ankle holster rode a light, 22-caliber Magnum six-shot revolver. On his right hip, he carried an eight-inch straight edge Japanese-style hari-kari blade knife. He'd cut thirty-three notches into the handle, telling the tale of the unlucky men it had stung. In his right pocket, he had a 38-caliber over and under two-shot Derringer. Lastly, he kept a set of brass knuckles in the top left pocket of his jacket.

He used the brass to convince people they should fear him. This weapon softened the hardest tough guys. When somebody owed something to someone, Jack was sent to collect. Those brass knuckles spoke loud and clear. They said, "Pay up or face the music."Black Jack always landed the first punch to the sternum, knocking the wind out of the person and making it difficult for them to breathe. The second punch knocked his victim out. If he were really pissed, he would hit him again, breaking the jawbone right next to the left ear lobe. The guy would eat through a straw for the next two months. Black Jack was a feared man and never cut anyone a break.

He watched every movement, straining to see this guy's hands. Don walked as if he didn't have a care in the world and this both puzzled and alarmed Black Jack. Don paid no notice to the old man. He was focused on the rhythmic clicking of his heels as he swung his arms, which enhanced the swagger of his shoulders. He was busy flirting with the woman behind the bar, and from her eyes intent upon his every move, it looked to him like his flirting was working.

The old man thought, *The fucker doesn't have anything that I can see.*

Don made it back to the bar in one piece, oblivious to his peril. He slid into a red leather swivel chair directly in front of the blond. "Gimme' a Sambuca with Grand Marnier on the rocks, please."

The barmaid made a questioning expression. *Huh, no one's ever asked me for that combination before. Oh well, the customer is always right.* She smiled, "Hi, I'm Alice. One Sambuca and Grand Marnier on the rocks coming right up."

Scooping a glass of ice, she free poured from both bottles simultaneously, filling the glass to the brim. The two liquids blended to a light golden drink that slid down Don's throat too easily. He pulled a dry Camel out of his pack and lit up.

Alice set a glass of ice water on the bar next to Don's drink. "This your first time here? I don't recall ever seeing you before." She smiled, "I woulda' remembered."

Don just raised his right eyebrow and smirked. "Well, I was kind of forced through the door because it was either swim, sink, or come in out of the storm."

The older man sitting in the corner with his back to the wall lit a new cigarette with the old snipe. Well-dressed in an expensive, blue sharkskin suit, his multi-colored silk tie flashed with a two-carat diamond stickpin, and his left hand sparkled with a pinky ring sporting a diamond so large it would have made a trophy wife blush. His black, out-of-a-bottle hair was razor styled into a "Mob cut," complementing his olive complexion. When he inhaled the smoke, it made his blood-shot, sleepless blue eyes water. He called out in a raspy, low voice, "Hey partner, gimme' another one."

Alice smiled, "Yes Sir, Mr. Roma!"

She slid back the mirrored door of the hidden compartment and reached inside to retrieve his private stock. He prided himself in having only the finest, the best of the best. Alice poured a three-shot glass, picked up a napkin, and took the drink to his table. "Thank you, Alice. Do me a favor and bring me the bottle and a glass."

"Sure thing, Mr. Roma."

When she brought his request, he said, "Thank you, Sweetie." He slid a sawbuck across the table.

"Thank you, Mr. Roma! You are so kind." She smiled and walked back to wait on Don at the bar. Mr. Roma kept watching Don as he bantered with Alice.

"This is a bad night to be walking the streets," she said. "In fact, this has been one of the worst winters since the blizzard of '88. Don't you think so?"

Don rolled his eyes and gulped down his drink as a flash of sadness flushed over him. "Yeah, I guess so. Gimme' another."

He slid the glass over to her. Alice refilled the glass, placing the drink on a new napkin. Don picked it up and held it in the air, "Here's to my father, George Ricci, who died in that storm. I guess who gives a fuck. I never saw him much anyway ... he was always too busy working."

With that, he shrugged and chugged down the whole glass of sweet hard liquor.

"Oh, I'm so sorry to hear that. My dad is dead, too. He had a heart attack and died in the subway." She looked misty eyed for just a moment and then said, "You ready for another?"

"Yeah, sure, fill it up."

Mr. Roma sat at his table, contemplating the problem that was haunting him. He'd been in the Mafia all of his adult life, and he had learned from his experiences. He had killed more men than he cared to remember. Some of them he didn't know; others had been his best friends and business associates.

He found it to be a piece of cake to snuff someone, from the first person he tried to rob. That guy mouthed off and Black Jack pushed the knife sideways past the ribs, with surprisingly little resistance, into his heart. The guy just gave Roma a funny look, buckled at the knees, closed his eyes, and dropped to the ground.

It was always this easy, no sweat. Roma never felt the slightest remorse for the killings. It was business and survival, that was all, with no option for failure. But with all of these hits, Mr. Roma had become a little paranoid. He figured someone, somewhere, sometime, would come along to give a little payback, in the form of his painful death.

Black Jack Roma kept his eyes glued to Don. He sucked hard, twice, putting a heater on the butt as he inhaled the smoke deep into his lungs. Swallowing a mouthful of liquor with a gulp, he exhaled through his nose and mouth at the same time. He resembled a snorting bull about to charge with the smoke flaring out. Once again, he inhaled and blew smoke rings one after another. Considered the cool thing to do when he first took up smoking as a street-punk kid, he never lost the habit.

Placing the revolver on the table, Black Jack called out, "Hey, you at the bar! Come here!"

Don heard him loud and clear. There was no one else in the bar except for the three of them, and he knew that the man was talking to him. But he kept talking and looking at Alice as if they were all alone. He hoped, if he ignored the man, he might just go away.

Black Jack called out again, “Hey, Asshole, I’m talkin’ to you! Get the fuck ova’ here, or I’ll just shoot you where you’re fuckin’ sittin’!”

Don bit his bottom lip, swung out of his bar chair, and began the long walk to this very threatening mobster’s table. He felt like his legs had weights on them; each step took effort. Normally Don wouldn’t be so fearful of an old man. But he knew even a little old man could be a violent threat with the equalizer of a gun in his hand. Don thought, *God, I’m going to get robbed by this hood.*

Black Jack didn’t say anything as he watched Don approach. Roma sized him up. He could smell fear coming from Don as a bead of sweat rolled down Don’s forehead and onto his cheek before it dripped to the floor with a soft patter. Black Jack held his cigarette in his lips with the lit tip pointing down. The smoke floated into his eyes and made him squint, which made him look even more menacing.

“Here, you can have my money,” Don said as he reached for his wallet in his left rear pocket.

“You reach back there and I’m gonna’ shoot you, you fucker! Who the fuck are ya’? Who sent ya’? What are ya’ doin’ here? Are ya’ packin’?”

Don just looked at him, speechless. He knew this man was mob connected and not to be screwed with. “You got me mixed up with someone else, Sir.” He held up his hands with open palms, “I just came in here because of the weather. I’ll ... I’ll leave right now! I just came in here to get outta’ the storm. No one sent me here!”

Black Jack raised the gun and pointed it at Don's midsection, "I said, are ya' packin'?"

"No ... no, I don't have any guns, just a knife! Please don't point that gun at me!"

Black Jack placed his thumb on the hammer and pulled down. The result was a slow click as the cylinder rotated, bringing a round into firing position. "Place ya' hands in the center of the table and lean forward."

"Yes Sir!" Don followed the instructions to a "T." Black Jack slid his chair back and raised himself slowly. He placed the gun against Don's spine in his lower back.

A chill ran up Don's back as he envisioned the gun going off, leaving him a cripple for life, if he lived. Black Jack then reached his hand under Don's left armpit, sliding it down to his waist and around to the front of his stomach, between his legs, and then slid his hand down his inner thigh to his ankle. Finding no weapons, he switched hands to check him on the other side. Black Jack kept the pistol on Don's spine and repeated the process. That's when he located the switchblade in Don's back pocket. Don breathed heavily; it had been a long time since he had been under another man's power to this extent.

"Wha'cha carrying a blade for?" Jack slipped the knife into his pocket.

"For protection."

"Protection from what?"

"Well, I guess from times like this."

"Oh really? Ya' wanna' stick me?"

"No Sir, I don't want to stick you."

Now satisfied, Jack sat down again and took another taste of his Chivas Regal. "Sit down before I knock ya' down."

"Can I go now?"

"No, Asshole, I just said to sit down!"

He took a seat as Black Jack poured a full glass of his finest for Don and another for himself. Sliding it over to him, Jack said, "Drink!"

Don kept looking at him in the eyes as he reached for the full glass.

Black Jack Roma changed his tone; he relaxed his demeanor as he spoke in a more friendly sounding voice. "Well, young fellow, who are you and what's your name?"

"I'm Don Ricci."

"Oh, you're Italian, so am I. What do you do?"

"Nothing much ... I really don't need to do anything."

This really piqued Jack's interest in this tough-looking young guy. "You rob banks or somethin'? What's your specialty?"

"I don't have any." Don thought, *This fuckin' guy thinks that I'm a hood.* Don smiled broadly, nodding his head. Something happened to his confidence; it soared as he got more bold. Sitting a little straighter in the chair, he took a mouthful of booze, swished it around his mouth, and swallowed. Getting a little drunker, he then reached over and poured himself another glass, as well as topping off Jack's. He drunkenly decided he'd brag and try to impress the old made man.

"I'm no bank robber. I've just done little shit, ya' know, but there was this one time when I saw a fuckin' smelly bum out mooching off of people, and something clicked. He pissed me off, you know?"

"Yeah, I know what you mean. So, what did you do?" Black Jack asked as he took a sip of whiskey.

"Well, you know Bostonians, nobody was paying attention, so I grab the guy, and said, 'Boston Police, fucker ... I'm arresting you for panhandling!' Then, I dragged him off down an alley."

Black Jack had been smiling, but now he was chuckling. "Fuck, I can see it all, ga' head, keep goin'."

"The stinking fuck tried to tell me he didn't have any money. I don't believe my own strength when I get mad. I pulled his pocket and the fuckin' thing ripped clean off his pants. So, I shove the wad in his face and say, 'You call this nothing?' Then, the stupid fuck has the nerve to ask for my badge!"

"Ha, ha, ha. That's rich. Keep goin'."

"So, then I beat the crap out of him so bad he left a smear of blood on the whitewashed bricks as he slid down the wall. It was kind of' pretty actually, like an abstract painting in the style of Jackson Pollack."

"Yea I heard of him. he was the guy that dumped paint on canvas and sold it for millions."

"I got eight hundred bucks and a nice buck knife out of the deal."

Both Don and Black Jack started to laugh hysterically.

"Don, you got something special, you know."

Don smiled. He became a little elated with the compliment.

"Don, tell me, you make your bones yet?"

A sheepish, almost-childlike smile crept across Don's face. "What do you mean? Did I ever kill someone?" he asked with a chuckle.

"That's just what I said, did ya' ever kill someone?"

Don put his finger into the drink, stirring slowly as he thought about this possibly incriminating question. He'd already run his drunken mouth about mugging the bum, but what if he had misjudged Black Jack? At least the mugging would carry a far lower penalty than confessing to murder. Then he stuck his finger into his mouth, withdrawing it slowly. This gave him a chance to think about it before answering.

"Yeah ... yeah, I did, just once."

This was just what Black Jack wanted to hear. He had pegged it just right. Smiling he said, "What happened? Tell me about it."

Don took out a cigarette and lit up. Again, this gave him a moment to gauge how much he wanted to tell a perfect stranger. Taking a drag, he inhaled deeply.

"Well ... this guy embarrassed me in front of some other people. He, ahh ... made me feel real bad. I don't like anyone making me feel bad. So, I got a bat, and I wanted to teach him some manners. But, I guess I got a little carried away and the next thing I realized, he was dead."

"So we got another Mickey Mantle here, is that right? Ha, ha, ha."

"You might say that."

"That's cool, I like that. You don't put up with no shit, do you?"

Don cocked his head, "Not if I can help it."

"You married, or got a girlfriend?"

"No, no."

"You gay?"

"NO, I'M NOT GAY!"

"Okay," he said, making a take-it-easy gesture with his hands, "I was just wonderin'."

Jack looked over to the bar. "Alice, baby. Give us another bottle."

Alice complied; walking over, she cracked open the bottle and poured as soon as she reached the table.

"Thanks, Sweetie." Jack kept pouring the liquor and after a while, he was getting some positive vibes about this new protégé.

"How would you like to work for me? I need an assistant. I could use a man with your talents."

"What would I have to do?"

"You'd have to go around to some businesses I've invested in. You'd pick up envelopes; that's all. I'm too busy doin' other stuff myself."

"That's it?"

"Yeah, that's it … for now."

Don paused, *Man I can't believe it. I come into this shit-hole and get a chance to work with the mob.*

"Don, are ya' interested in an opportunity to fill my shoes? The hours are short and the green backs are more than the average man would make in a lifetime."

"It sounds good to me."

"After a while, ya' would garner the same respect that I have. Just think, kid ... ya' could be somebody!"

"That's the salary?"

"Don't worry about the salary. You'll be making more fuckin' money than you can spend. Just don't fuck with me and you won't have no worries. You understand?"

"Can I think about it?"

"Sure, take ya' time. When ya' ready, ya' come and see me, and we'll get to work! Okay? I'll see ya' soon!"

This chance meeting with Mr. Roma became Don Ricci's introduction into mob life and underworld contract killing. Black Jack Roma continued asking the questions, and Don Ricci continued answering them until the sun shone through the red, white, and blue-leaded glass.

Don was three sheets to the wind when he finally staggered into a brisk chill of a late winter morning. The frozen slush crunched under Don's boots as he stumbled his way to his vehicle. He found his car buried in snow and ice from the plows. "Son of a bitch! Will you look what those dirty bastards did to my fuckin' car!"

He kicked at the ice and snow that covered his car until he was able to open the driver's door. Starting it, he turned on the heat and watched the frozen covering melt off the glass. Don sat there thinking about the night. *What's my next step?*

That was when he spied part of a parking ticket sticking through the ice. Rage kicked in as if this was the most degrading thing that had ever happened to him. "You fuckin' asshole, what the fuck are you doin' to me!"

He jumped out of the car and pulled the citation off the windshield wiper blade, ripping it into shreds. He picked those up again and threw them down, stomping on them. An afterthought hit him as he tried to find the ticket writer's name and badge number on the remnants.

"Who the fuck was the son of a bitch that gave me that fuckin' ticket!" After looking for the name, he found it was illegible and blurred from the melted snow.

Flashing back to his night that took an unexpected turn into surrealism, he recalled the conversation that killed a fifth of smooth-drinking whiskey. As they parted, the older man shook his hand and gave him a slap on the shoulder. With that, Black Jack Roma strolled out the back door and disappeared down the streets of the combat zone.

Epilogue:
The Letter

Don was sitting in the leather chair looking out to the backyard. The sun played on the floor with heated beams displaying the dust floating on the currents of hot air bouncing off the dark oak floors. He was in deep thought about Julie. His lips were drawn tight in against his teeth. He had many mixed feelings for her and of her. Breathing deeply, he fantasized about her essence passing up his nose and inhaling deep down into his lungs. He could remember her taste and her warm, sensual aroma.

Glancing over to the bottle of Canadian Leaf Whiskey, his mouth started to salivate as he envisioned the golden liquid washing over his taste buds. Walking over to the bar, he took a large tumbler and filled it halfway. The chugging of the booze from the bottle sent a vapor of alcohol into the air. It was a fine art of devouring the products of fermentation.

He sniffed the consistency of the contents of the glass and took a full sip, washing the drink over his tongue and inhaling the fumes at the same time. After the second glass, he decided to write a short letter to Julie on the subject of his feelings of indifference:

My Dear Julie,

This is our anniversary, "HAPPY ANNIVERSARY."

You left me when I needed you the most. We were starting to understand each other after such a rocky start. You were being transformed into the perfect woman for me. Didn't I show you how much I cared for you? I took you because I loved you and needed you and you needed me. Did I punish you when you attacked me with the bailing hook?

Well, it is over between us. You saw to that by your actions. You will never know when we walk past each other in the street. You will never know if you sit next to me in a darkened theater. You will never know if I serve food to you in a restaurant. You will never know who I am, where I am and when I will be seeing you.

Good-bye, or as the Europeans say, " 'Till we meet again, maybe."

Don smiled a dreamy smile and took a large gulp of whisky, swishing it around his mouth as if it were mouthwash, swallowing it, and blowing the fumes into the air.

***

"Oh God, I am so dog-tired. It's been such a long day. I'll see you tomorrow, Barb."

Barb looked up at Julie and smiled. "You take care of yourself dear. I'm going to go home and crash myself right after I cook dinner for my hubby and clean up the house."

Julie rolled her eyes and mumbled, "Thank God I don't have anybody that I have to be a servant to."

Walking to the parking lot, she spoke to herself, "Such a pleasant spring day." She turned to face the sun, closing her eyes, and stood there for a short time.

She suddenly heard Barbara say, "You okay?"

Julie snapped back to the moment. Barbara was looking at her with a questioning expression written all over her face.

"Yes Barb, thank you. You are so sweet to ask. I was just soaking up the warmth. It was very kind of you to be so concerned."

Turning around and waving, Barbara disappeared inside.

"There is so much goodness in the world," Julie said. "We still have so much to look forward to with companions like her."

Julie approached the car and checked the back seat, per the instructions of Joe. All was clear, as it should be. Pulling out onto the street, she was ever conscious of the other cars.

She turned the wheel of the used SUV that she had bought at Joe's suggestion. He advised her to change as much of her modus operandi as possible to that of someone very different. She was just trying to work on getting life back to normal.

Pulling into the driveway, she glanced at the flag of her mailbox, which was in the upright position. Julie didn't remember putting it up when she left home in the morning. Parking the car, she casually walked to the front of the house to check the mail.

Opening the box, she found utility bills and too much junk mail, but at the bottom of the stack was an envelope void of any writing. There was no stamp, no return address, or anything to identify who sent it. Slowly, she strolled up the front walkway, ripping the envelope open and sitting down on the warm, sun baked red bricks. It gave her a safe feeling to be in the sunlight.

"Huh, just some more junk mail I bet." Unfolding the paper, Julie's eyes widened as she started to shake with fear. Dropping the house keys, she awkwardly snapped them up and spun around, looking quickly in every direction. Despite trembling, she managed to insert the key into the front door and found some sense of safety by slamming it quickly. She didn't have to think for a moment who she would call.

"Joe, Joe I just got a letter from him!"

"Who's him?"

"The Master."

"Julie, I'm coming right now. I will be there in a few minutes."

Off in the distance, she could hear a siren with the decibels changing as he got closer.

Adrenaline raced through Joe. His anxiety built as he raced to protect Julie. This was no longer professional for him; it had become personal. The Master threatened a woman he hesitated to admit he had become infatuated with. He pulled up to the curb with the siren blasting loudly.

Normally, when responding to a call about bad guys breaking the law, Joe would slip up with the siren off. In this case, though, he wanted to chase away anyone lurking near Julie's house that might harm her.

Julie was halfway down the walkway when Joe jumped out of the car. She lunged into his arms for safety. He consoled her by saying, "It's okay, Julie. I'm here … you're safe."

As a professional law enforcement officer, and she a victim of a crime he was investigating, they had both maintained an emotional distance as their friendship had grown.

But in this moment that the Master had once again become a real rather than theoretical threat, for the first time they let their emotional guard drop as they walked into the house, she clinging to him as he protected her in his arms. Silently, each acknowledged life-changing feelings for the other.

"Joe, here's the letter that he put in my mailbox." She handed it to Joe, who held it by the edge of the paper as he read it.

THE END OF BOOK ONE AND THE PRELUDE OF BOOK TWO

Chapter One

Little Joey

Black Jack walked into Bobby's Diner on Revere Street for some bacon and eggs after having just finished a payback job.

Little Joey would not be fucking Black Jack, or anyone else, anymore.

Joseph Garza had opened a fruit store in Charlestown with the stolen proceeds he skimmed off of the daily take when he and Black Jack were partners. The little man thought that all was forgotten, but memories last a lifetime. It had been ten years since Black Jack had last seen him, and to tell the truth, Jack had really put him out of his mind.

Black Jack inhaled the tasty Lonsdale Vintage smoke of a rare smuggled Cuban cigar as he drove his black Cadillac convertible down the dimly lit streets of Everett. He took a short cut down a side street, just for a change of scenery, as he headed to the North End for an espresso coffee at one of the mob's pastry shops.

The car was not traveling more than twenty miles per hour. No need to rush at this time of the morning. The road was empty but for a few trucks making early deliveries. Every place of business was closed but with its night-lights on; this was to discourage break-ins.

Except for one 24-hour store that was owned and run by Little Joey Garza.

All of the memories came rushing back when he saw Joey standing out front of the store. Black Jack touched the brakes gently, stopping in the middle of the street.

Joey looked up, smiling. He thought, *hey, here is some business.* He called out, "Hey, need some coffee? I just made a pot … I'll throw in a fresh donut for zip."

"Don't mind if I do," Black Jack said.

He cut the wheel into the parking space. The high beams lit up the stairs and blinded Little Joey.

Joey held up his left hand to shade his eyes. His glasses sat punched on the tip of his nose. As always, he had a three-day beard under his unkempt mustache. He wore a butcher's apron that was meant for a larger man. It went down to his worn-out work boots that held his tiny feet.

Black Jack turned the motor off and sat there for a moment, looking at Joey. All of the old resentments flooded back into his mind as Black Jack reached under the front seat, taking hold of the shopping bag that was stashed away for just a moment like this.

Joey did not recognize the man getting out of the car. It has been a long time and people change; some lose weight and others gain. Black Jack had gained; he also had been lifting weights to increase his strength to spite his age. With the Cuban stuck in his right cheek, he put the bag under his left armpit as he walked past the little shit.

"Hey, Joey. How are you doin'?"

Joey stopped smiling. The muscles in his face dropped, making him look like Emmett Kelly.

Black Jack said, "How's business, Joey?"

"Oh, I can't complain … but things could be better. How about yourself?"

"Good … good, very good. Joey … seeing you again makes me very happy. I really forgot just how much I fuckin' hate you, you little fuckin' little prick, you thief."

"What do you mean?"

"You ripped me off. You ripped your partner off. After I took you in – treated you like a brother. I think it's time for you and me to be partners once again. I'll be stopping by every week for my share of the vig. Let's see, what would be fair?"

Joey just stood there, looking bug eyed.

"What did you say, Joey? You think that a grand a week would be fair? Okay, I agree with you. A grand a week, you can make your first payment … up front," Black Jack raised his voice, "NOW!"

Joey's mouth was foaming as he started to speak. "Who the fuck do you think you are? You come in my store, trying to strong arm … me? You fuckin' asshole!"

Joey reached for the closest weapon that he could find. He grabbed a can of wedding soup off the shelf. "Get the fuck out of here before I fuckin' kill you, you fuckin' big pile of shit!"

Joey raised the can over his head, acting like David against Goliath.

Black Jack had his arms crossed with the bag in his right hand. "Ok Joey … sorry to have bothered you. I'll leave then."

He stepped forward. At the same time, the bag came flying with such speed that all Joey saw was a flash as the rubber-covered copper cable struck Little Joey on his left jaw. Joey's head followed the cable towards the door with a loud cracking sound. Blood gushed out past the foam, ending up on the doorframe.

Joey dropped the can to the floor, and then grabbed and cradled his jaw. He didn't make a sound or utter a word.

He was tougher and more violent than Black Jack, just smaller. But this time Black Jack had the upper hand as he struck Joey again on his right shoulder and then on his left. This prevented any reprisal from the little shit.

Black Jack said, "Joey I'm going to say it again, do we have an agreement?" Raising his voice once again, he said, "WELL, DO WE?"

Joey's eyes now looked really pissed. He could have killed Black Jack with that stare. With a muffled sound, he said, "You go fuck yourself."

Black Jack now let the bloody bag fall to the floor. It was then that Joey saw what had happened and that Mr. Copper Rod had slapped him.

Black Jack smacked him again across the forehead, snapping his head and almost making it touch his back. Joey fell to the floor unconscious. Closing the front door, he turned off the lights, and then grabbed Joey's shirt collar, dragging him into the back of the store for more enlightenment.

Reaching behind his back, he took out two pairs of handcuffs from their pouches. He cuffed Joey's arms behind him and shackled his feet.

Putting on a pair of rubber gloves, he then went to work looking for any cash and valuables. He emptied the register, and then searched the cooler behind the counter for additional hidden cash. In it he found a paper lunch bag with four rolls of green being held by thick rubber bands.

Placing the bag by the front door, he walked back into the storage room just as Little Joey was coming around. He looked at Black Jack with the same evil stare, as if he had the upper hand of the situation.

"Joey, I found the cash in the cooler. Where is the rest of the green?"

Picking him up with ease, Black Jack placed him in a swivel chair.

Joey said, "I ain't got nuthin' else. Just that and what's in the cash register. My arms are killing me. Take these fuckin' cuffs off."

"Sure … sure, Joey, as soon as you tell me where the rest of it is. Is it in the walk-in cooler, Joey?"

As he swung the cooler's heavy door open, he started to look in all of the regular places that someone would hide valuables. Black Jack started sweating after making a mess of the cooler and finding nothing. He picked up the copper again and faced Little Joey once more.

"Joey, I'll ask you again. Are you going to tell me?"

"What do you want from me, huh? What do you want?"

"Where's the money? What, you don't understand? Do you speak English? Maybe you need a little more convincing, huh … you little prick."

Black Jack removed the skinning knife from its sheath that was right behind his hip holster. Raising it over his head, he stabbed Joey in his left shoulder blade. Electric shock shot to Joey's brain as he realized that he had been knifed.

Joey screamed out with pain and fear, "Don't kill me! Don't kill me, please! I ain't got anything else, honest to God as my witness."

"Joey. You're too fuckin' loud. People are going to hear you."

Black Jack left the knife sticking in Joey's shoulder as he opened a utility drawer.

"Ah, there's what the doctor ordered."

Grabbing a roll of duct tape, he wrapped it around Joey's chin, going up and down, round and round again, wrapping his jaw tight. He was unable to open his mouth to scream, but he was able to communicate – somewhat.

Black Jack asked once again, "Where is the money?"

Joey said something, but Black Jack could not understand the muffled words. He pushed the handle of the knife, turning it as if it were a screwdriver. The pain of the blade cutting into the bone was more than he could take.

He whined, "Okay … okay, I'll tell you."

"What did you say, you little prick?"

Black Jack put all of his weight on the handle of the knife as it sank into the bone and popped out the other side, all the way up to the hilt of the knife. Once more, he twisted it hard as Joey screamed out a muffled cry. Black Jack left the blade sticking in the bone, unable to go any deeper. He walked in front of Joey and knelt down on his right knee. He reached for Joey's chin, lifting his head.

His eyes were not so defiant anymore. They were more sorrowful, suggesting that he was now a more wise, prudent, and repentant man for his past indiscretions.

Asking once again, rhythmically, "Where … is … your … cash … in … your … stash? Hey, that rhymes. I'm a poet and didn't know it."

Joey pointed with his head to the corner. In a muffled voice, he said, "Over there."

Black Jack got up slowly, walking to the corner. There were three cases of tomatoes stacked. He stopped, and then looked back at Joey.

"Where!"

Painfully, he uttered, "Under the tomatoes."

Black Jack set them aside. Picking up a steel plate revealed a safe in the floor.

"What's the combination?"

Joey said something, but Black Jack didn't understand a sound. Walking over, he ripped the tape off of his head, painfully taking a patch of hair with it.

"Now … do you care to repeat that again?"

Joey was in torment from the pain of the knife that was still in his shoulder. "Turn right to 10 three times … left to 60 twice … right to 80 once … left to zero … then lift the door."

Black Jack did as he was instructed; lifting the lid to the safe revealed neat stacks of cash with a small box sitting on top. It was a typical jeweler's box with blue fuzz, four inches square. He opened it to find it filled with loose cut diamonds. He gave a very long whistle.

"Hey Joey, who did you fuck out of these?"

Joey was getting that evil look once again – the kind that goes right through you – the look that is supposed to put fear into your soul, making you tremble for mercy. The only problem was that Joey was bound in iron and couldn't do shit.

Black Jack filled a large shopping bag with the cash, placing the diamonds on top. He put them at the front door next to the smaller bag that was already there. Casually walking back to the rear of the store, he spoke aloud to Joey.

"Joey, now we got that settled, I'll just lay claim to all of that shit at the front door. We'll call it even … for the cash you stole from me. Is that okay with you?"

Joey whispered loudly because of being weak, "Do you think that I'm going to let you fuck over me and do nothing … do you? If you do, you're more of a fuckin' ass-hole that I thought you were."

"Joey, you don't seem to understand, do you? I just robbed you and stabbed you. Now, you are going to pay me one grand a week. What don't you understand?"

"Fuck you. I'm coming after you … you fuckin' bastard … I'm going to give you some payback!"

"Okay, Joey … you can't say that I didn't give you a chance … to make things right."

From the counter, Black Jack picked up a twelve-inch butcher knife. He held it in his right hand with the point almost halfway down his leg. Grabbing Joey's hair, he pulled his head back. Coughing from his lungs and clearing his throat, Black Jack spat phlegm into Joey's face.

Joey shouted, "You cocksucker!"

He spat back at Black Jack in reprisal, but when he did, it gushed red blood, spraying into Black Jack's face. The butcher knife entered Joey's chin, passing through his throat, nasal passage, and brain, exiting the skull. It stopped only because the hilt pushed Joey's mouth shut when it met the jawbone. There was an almost comical expression on Joey's face that lingered for just a few moments. His eyes were strangely open, looking at Black Jack.

Black Jack and Joey almost touched noses while Jack peered deeply into his eyes as the spirit left, leaving a shell behind. They glazed over with a blank stare. Without moving away, Black Jack said, whispering, "Hey Joe … Joey, you there?"

Joey exhaled a foul last breath, and Black Jack inadvertently inhaled at the same time, consuming the foul taste. Jack coughed as if to dispel Joey's last attack.

Jack stood up, and looking down at the body, he removed the blade and cleaned it off on Joey's apron. He turned toward the door with his back to the body and said, "Hey Joey, that's all she wrote … Ha, Ha, Ha, Ha."

JOIN THE CONVERSATION

Contact the Author at:
donricciwiseguy@aol.com

Join the Fan Discussion at:
www.facebook.com/DonRicciWiseGuy

If you liked the book, please remember to write a review on the Amazon and Barnes and Noble websites.

To be notified when the SEQUEL is available for purchase, please email to the address above or "Like" us on Facebook.

Acknowledgments

I would like to thank the following people:

Laura Tichy-Smith, my editor, who guided me through my first novel and who is already working on my second novel, "Don Ricci: Apprentice."

Deborah, my wife, who first believed in me and gave me the motivation to put my thoughts on the computer screen.

Don Brock, who listened so intently to my readings and suggested that I join the Crossed Quills writers' group in Naples, Florida.

John Forbes, who gave me permission to let my characters come to life on the written page regardless, and in spite, of their antics.

Rose, my sister, who always encouraged me throughout my life.

Create Space, who has guided me through my publication.

To know more about Anthony V. Aqua or *Don Ricci*, you may email donricciwiseguy@aol.com.

About the Author

Anthony V. Aqua hales from Boston's North End where he grew up helping his father, who was the first-generation child (born in Anita, Pennsylvania) of Sicilian immigrants, with his olive oil business. He went to boarding school in Andover, Massachusetts, where he learned to fear God, and the "French Canadian brothers." His former career as a police officer provided him with insights and anecdotes that now inspire his writing.

He currently lives in Naples, Florida, with his wife as well as with his best friend, Clara, his Yorkie.

Made in the USA
Lexington, KY
25 July 2014